M

Sa

Meet pediatri___ ___ ___ ___ ___ ___ n
and his estranged son, paramedic Jonno Morgan,
who is no stranger to living life on the edge.
But for these two men, their lives will never
be the same when nurse Elsie and trainee
paramedic Brie enter their worlds.

Secret Son to Change His Life

Seven years ago, Brie's dreams came true when
she spent one fun night with Jonno before he was
due to leave. And then her life was rocked when
she discovered she was pregnant, and her son had
spina bifida. Now Jonno's back and she can finally
reveal the secret she's been longing to tell him…

How to Rescue the Heart Doctor

When Anthony Morgan's relationship with his
son broke down, he felt the hole in his life would
never be replaced. Until nurse Elsie walks into his
operating room! But she is the protective mother
of Brie and grandmother to his newly discovered
grandson. Will finding each other lead to
the second chance they never thought they
would have?

*Don't miss this hugely emotional generational duet
where happy families are made!*

*Both books are available now
from Harlequin Medical Romance*

Dear Reader,

Links between characters are the foundation of any story, but it's a bonus for me when I can both read and write links that span more than one book. I love that I can not only follow other people I've met into their own stories, but I get glimpses of what's happening to the people I already know and love.

I'm also excited about exploring a totally new link in the second book of this duo, an intergenerational one, with Anthony and Elsie's story being my first romance between an older couple. I know from experience that being older is no barrier to falling in love and finding happiness. It can, in fact, be even more special.

This duo may be centered on fathers and sons, but it's the women in these two books—Brie and her mother, Elsie—who are the catalysts for these stories, and I hope you love them as much as I do.

Happy reading,

Alison xxx

HOW TO RESCUE
THE HEART DOCTOR

—

ALISON ROBERTS

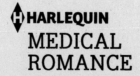

HARLEQUIN
**MEDICAL
ROMANCE**

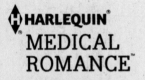

HARLEQUIN®
MEDICAL
ROMANCE™

Recycling programs
for this product may
not exist in your area.

ISBN-13: 978-1-335-73769-4

How to Rescue the Heart Doctor

Copyright © 2023 by Alison Roberts

For questions and comments about the quality of this book,
please contact us at CustomerService@Harlequin.com.

Harlequin Enterprises ULC
22 Adelaide St. West, 41st Floor
Toronto, Ontario M5H 4E3, Canada
www.Harlequin.com

Printed in U.S.A.

Alison Roberts has been lucky enough to live in the South of France for several years recently but is now back in her home country of New Zealand. She is also lucky enough to write for the Harlequin Medical Romance line. A primary school teacher in a former life, she later became a qualified paramedic. She loves to travel and dance, drink champagne, and spend time with her daughter and her friends. **Alison Roberts** is the author of over one hundred books!

Books by Alison Roberts

Harlequin Medical Romance

Morgan Family Medics
Secret Son to Change His Life

Two Tails Animal Refuge
The Vet's Unexpected Family

Royal Christmas at Seattle General
Falling for the Secret Prince

Christmas Miracle at the Castle
Miracle Baby, Miracle Family
A Paramedic to Change Her Life
One Weekend in Prague
The Doctor's Christmas Homecoming

Visit the Author Profile page
at Harlequin.com for more titles.

PROLOGUE

Just a day or two before…

IT WAS FIVE O'CLOCK in the morning, the staff-room was empty and the full pot of coffee on the automatic percolator was too tempting to resist after the long night that paediatric cardiac surgeon, Anthony Morgan, had just had. A quiet moment to sit down and enjoy a mug of hot, strong coffee was exactly what he needed.

Only seconds later, however, a nurse came in carrying a baby in her arms and he couldn't blame her for looking so taken aback to see him there.

'I'm not in your way, am I? I can go…' He put his mug of coffee down on the low table beside the chair he was sitting in, but some-how he managed to tip its contents onto the pile of folded newspaper on the tabletop. He couldn't quite stifle his weary groan.

'Don't worry about it.' The tone of the nurse's voice was kind. 'That paper's due to go into the recycle bin anyway. And don't get up. Please. You look like you need a quiet space even more than Tommy and I do, Mr Morgan.'

'Please, call me Anthony...'

'I'm Elsie, I've just started recently on this ward. I've seen you around before, of course, but not usually at silly o'clock.'

She had a rather lovely smile. She also had silvery grey streaks in her hair that told him she was older than most of the nurses here at St Nick's.

'It has been rather a long night,' Anthony admitted. 'I've been in PICU since midnight with a wee girl who looked like she might not make it. She had a fairly major surgery today and ran into problems with arrhythmias that put her into acute heart failure.'

'Oh... I'm sorry.' She was frowning but then looked shocked. 'It wasn't Victoria, was it? I knew she was having her surgery yesterday.' He could see her almost wince as she realised she was stepping over privacy boundaries. 'Sorry,' she said again. 'I shouldn't have asked. It's just that I spent some time talking to Vicky's mother the last time I was on duty.

I'm helping to raise a grandson with spina bifida so we had a connection. And Vicky's just an adorable little girl. She gives the best cuddles in the world—just like my Felix.'

He was catching undercurrents to her words. She was a grandmother? What was it that made her want to be doing shift work? But he'd been right about the kindness he could hear in her voice. She'd taken the time to connect with not only a young patient but with her family and, with experience of a child with special needs, she would have been able to do that better than most. She also clearly adored her grandson. Anthony found himself smiling. He didn't have to keep any barriers up. Vicky would hopefully be back on the ward within a very short space of time. This nurse was part of his own team, wasn't she?

'She's okay. She's a wee fighter. Her cardiologist has got her electrolyte balance sorted now so she may well come onto the ward in the next day or two and you might be able to get another one of those cuddles. Is your grandson the same age?'

'No, he's six—a couple of years older. We've been through a few surgeries ourselves but nothing as serious as an open-heart procedure.'

'I'm glad he hasn't needed it.' Anthony managed to stifle a yawn. 'I don't actually need to be here for Vicky any longer, but if I went home I would no sooner get there than I'd have to turn around and fight my way through rush-hour traffic to come back. I've got a full Theatre list this morning so I thought I'd put my feet up here instead. And have a strong coffee.' He glanced down at the empty mug in his hand. 'So much for that plan.'

He saw Elsie shift the weight of the baby in her arms, who looked to be soundly asleep. 'Here…give that to me.' She held her hand out for the mug. 'I'm well practised in making a coffee one-handed. Why don't you put the newspaper in the recycle bin by the fridge?'

'Sure.' Anthony started to gather up the sections of the paper.

'How do you take your coffee?'

'Black, thanks. No sugar.'

He put the last section of the newspaper on top of the pieces he was already holding. It was the front page, with the banner at the top, a date of a few days ago and a photograph of a rescue helicopter with a backdrop of mountains. There was a man standing beside the stretcher about to be loaded into the aircraft. A hero who'd helped save the life of an injured climber.

Anthony couldn't look away. He couldn't even take a breath because it felt as if his chest was being squeezed in a vice. How long had it been since he'd seen this man's face in real life? Nearly ten years? How long had it been since he'd felt welcome in his life? Probably not since his mother's funeral even longer ago.

Until he heard her speak, he'd barely registered that Elsie had put a fresh mug of coffee down on the table beside him. Or that she was sitting down herself. Watching him.

'Do you know him?' Her voice was soft this time. A little tentative, perhaps. 'Is he a relative of yours?'

Anthony still didn't look up from the photograph. He shouldn't say anything but the words seemed to get torn out of a deep place in his chest.

'Yeah… Jonathon Morgan is my son.'

Why on earth had he told a complete stranger something that personal? It might be nearly twenty years but he'd never forgotten what it had been like to be the hot topic of gossip on the hospital grapevine.

Anthony dropped the paper and rubbed at his forehead. 'Sorry,' he murmured. 'Maybe the night's been longer than I realised. I'm quite sure you don't want to hear about my personal life.' He pasted a smile on his face. 'Families, huh?' He reached for his coffee. 'They can be complicated, can't they?'

The sound Elsie made suggested that she had no desire to hear any more about his personal life. Or maybe this had suddenly become awkward because she already knew about that old scandal? Anthony focused on the smell and taste of his coffee to avoid any eye contact.

It was a relief when the baby she was holding woke up and started crying miserably. It was even more of a relief when Elsie got up and excused herself.

Left alone, Anthony drank his coffee, his gaze drifting back to that front page photograph. That tightness in his chest was still there, along with a twinge that felt like a very familiar pain.

So Jonno was back in the country…

The son who wanted nothing to do with him…

Anthony drained his mug and got to his feet. He was ready to deal with this the way he'd dealt with unpleasant emotional issues for far longer than he cared to remember. By focusing on the problems of others that he could potentially fix. Medical problems to do with little hearts that were broken in some physical way.

He could feel a wry smile teasing the corners of his mouth as he quietly left this ward staffroom. How ironic was it that his own heart had been broken by something that couldn't be fixed?

CHAPTER ONE

Uh-oh...

Luckily, Elsie Henderson saw him before he saw her so probably had time to avoid getting any closer. Anthony Morgan had his back to her, in fact, as he spoke to someone behind the main desk of this cardiac surgical ward.

Did she have time to take Vicky, the small girl who was balanced on her hip with her arms around her nurse's neck, back to her bed? It was quite possible that Mr Morgan was coming to see Vicky, who was one of his patients, but Elsie didn't want him to see *her.*

She'd only met the man for the first time a couple of days ago but she knew something about him that he *didn't* know.

Something very personal.

Something he had the right to know.

But Elsie wasn't sure she had the right to

tell him and she'd been wrestling with the dilemma ever since.

The split second of indecision about how to avoid a face-to-face encounter in the ward corridor was almost too long. As Elsie was turning to go back in the direction she'd come from, she could see in her peripheral vision that Anthony was turning as well. Towards her. She stared at the open door to the playroom she had just come out of.

'Let's go back in here for a second, darling. I don't think I showed you what was inside the Wendy house, did I? Do you know there's a little stove with an oven door that actually opens?'

Vicky shook her head but her eyes were drifting shut. 'I want to go back to bed,' she told Elsie. 'I feel funny...'

'Do you?' Elsie was now safely screened by a tall bookshelf in the play area but an alarm bell was ringing at the back of her head for a different reason this time. 'What sort of funny, darling?'

Vicky was a few days past open heart surgery to repair congenital defects. She'd only come back from the intensive care unit yesterday but, in the astonishing way children were capable of bouncing back from even major surgery, she had desperately wanted to get out of bed to play. It was only the side rails that were raised on her bed that had thwarted her attempt to climb out.

'How 'bout I go and get you an ice cream?' her mother, Julie, had suggested. 'I'm pretty sure I saw your favourite kind in a freezer in the cafeteria. The one with the strawberry jelly in the middle?'

'And I could take you for a little walk while Mummy's gone,' Elsie had suggested. 'Just for a couple of minutes. Maybe we could have a look at the playroom for when you get better. No walking yet, though, and we'll have to be very careful. I can find a wheelchair for you or I can carry you. Which would you like better?'

Vicky had held her arms up in the air by way of response, a wide smile on her face, and Julie had given Elsie a grateful smile. Maybe the young mother needed a few minutes to herself after days of intense anxiety about her daughter. Elsie had bonded with both Vicky and Julie when the little girl had been first admitted to have all her pre-surgical tests and checks done. Heart issues were only one of the challenges Vicky was facing in life. She'd also been born with spina bifida—a birth defect that Elsie had become an expert in over the years since her own grandson had also been born with the condition so her connection with both Vicky and Julie had been instant.

As a nurse, she was also an expert in sensing when something wasn't right and she could hear an odd note in Vicky's voice. She could also see how pale that little face was becoming.

'My head's going…roundy roundy.' Vicky had to stop to take a breath after only a few words and then she coughed. '*Ow…*' She sounded close to tears now. 'It *hurts…*'

Okay… Any personal preferences became totally irrelevant as Elsie moved swiftly back towards the doors into the main corridor. She wasn't worried about seeing Anthony Morgan now. She would welcome seeing him. Or anyone else who might be in a position to assist her.

Because something was going wrong. Fast enough to be frightening.

She could feel Vicky slumping in her arms. Was her level of consciousness dropping? Her respiration rate had certainly increased. Her small patient was almost gasping.

'What's happening?' Anthony Morgan was

only a few steps away as Elsie stepped into the corridor and he must have seen the fear in her eyes. 'Is that Vicky?'

'Something's wrong,' Elsie said. 'Her LOC's dropping. She's short of breath…'

'This way…' Anthony put a hand on her shoulder, guiding her across the corridor and into the ward's treatment room that had a bed in the middle and was lined with cupboards and shelves stacked with all the medical equipment and supplies that could be needed for even major procedures and emergencies. 'Put her on the bed.'

Anthony unhooked the stethoscope from around his neck as Elsie laid Vicky on the bed. He slid the disc under a pink pyjama top that had a sparkly picture of a unicorn on the front.

'Her heart sounds are a bit muffled,' he said moments later. 'And she's tachycardic at one forty. See if you can find a radial pulse?' He put his hand on Vicky's head, smoothing her hair back. 'Hey, Vicky…can you open your eyes?'

Vicky's eyelashes fluttered, which suggested she could hear him, but she didn't open her eyes. She was opening and closing her mouth, however, in an increasing struggle to get enough oxygen. She looked like a fish out of water, Elsie thought as she tried to find a radial pulse in the tiny wrist she was holding between her fingers and thumb.

'I can't feel a pulse.' Elsie was surprised at how calm her voice sounded when she could feel the claws of panic digging in, deep in her gut. Vicky's blood pressure could be dangerously low.

'Bring the defibrillator trolley over. We need to get an ECG and a blood pressure if we can. I might need an airway adjunct as well.' Anthony was frowning heavily. 'Her jugular veins aren't distended but with muffled heart sounds and being hypotensive, it could be Beck's triad forming.' He glanced up at Elsie as she pushed the trolley closer, to see if she understood the reference.

She did. And it was enough to make her swallow hard. 'Cardiac tamponade?'

Bleeding into the pericardial space around the heart was a well-recognised complication following cardiac surgery. It could also be dangerous because, if it happened rapidly, it could be enough to stop the heart functioning well before they'd have time to get her back to Theatre.

Anthony nodded when Elsie reached for

the defibrillator pads first, rather than any electrodes to record a more detailed ECG or a cuff to measure blood pressure. She helped him remove the unicorn pyjama top and stick them on but they could both feel the change as Vicky crashed and stopped breathing. Anthony barely waited for the static on the screen of the defibrillator to settle and confirm a rhythm of ventricular fibrillation—incompatible with life—before he hit the red 'cardiac arrest' button on the wall to summon urgent help.

Elsie grabbed the bag mask unit from the trolley but Anthony took it from her hands to hold over Vicky's mouth and nose himself. He tipped her head back and squeezed the bag, watching the chest rise and fall.

'Shall I start chest compressions?' Elsie was poised, flashes of a recent training session to keep nursing staff up-to-date with CPR protocols foremost in her brain.

Place the heel of one hand in the centre of the chest.

Keep your arm straight and elbow locked.

Push hard and fast with a ratio of thirty compressions to two breaths.

Except…this little girl was only just beginning to heal after major heart surgery. How much damage could be done by pushing hard on that fragile-looking chest with its sutures still in place under the clear adhesive dressing?

Anthony Morgan must have seen the question in her eyes. 'Hold off on compressions. We'll shock first. What's her current weight, do you know?'

'It was almost twenty kilograms this morning.' More than a healthy weight for a four-year-old girl but it was a common problem with children who had major mobility issues.

'Charge to forty joules, then,' Anthony instructed. 'We'll go to eighty if we need to repeat.'

Elsie held her breath as the defibrillator's whine changed to a strident beeping to announce that the charge was set.

'Stand clear,' she warned, watching to make sure Anthony lifted his hands and that his body was not touching the bed, before she pushed the discharge button. She felt herself wince as Vicky's tiny body jerked with even the small jolt of electricity going through her heart.

'Still in VF.' Anthony's voice was calm as he watched the screen. 'Charge again. Eighty joules this time, please.'

Elsie adjusted the setting, thankful that the training session had included practice with the latest models of defibrillators like this one. She was even more thankful that more staff were arriving in response to the urgent summons of a cardiac arrest alarm. She recognised an anaesthetist, who immediately took over airway control and oxygenation, a paediatric cardiologist and Laura, one of this ward's most senior nurses. The mobile arrest team arrived shortly afterwards, pushing two more trolleys laden with equipment.

These people were all far more experienced than Elsie in dealing with an emergency like this but, as she stepped back with the intention of leaving, Laura shook her head.

'Stay,' she said. 'Watch and learn…and we might need a runner…'

So Elsie stayed, watching the team sort themselves into positions under Anthony's leadership. Because he was the cardiothoracic surgeon and the decision had already been made to perform a resternotomy and reopen that small chest. If it was a tamponade that had caused the cardiac arrest, the pressure had to be released as quickly as possible to have any chance of saving Vicky's life. There was no time to take her to Theatre.

Anthony and one other doctor had ripped open sterile packs and were donning gowns, gloves, hats and masks. Someone else took a folded drape, pressed the centre of it onto Vicky's chest and then unfolded each side. The little girl that Elsie had been talking to and holding in her arms only minutes ago vanished beneath the sterile green cloth, her entire body covered. Only her chest was visible through the clear plastic adhesive window as a kit of instruments was emptied onto the sterile field. The strings of Anthony's gown were still being tied by Laura as he reached for a scalpel. His assistant picked up something that looked like a pair of pliers.

It should have made this easier to watch by creating a distance that made it possible to focus simply on a potentially life-saving procedure and not something ultimately invasive that was happening to a small human that Elsie had been able to bond with all too easily as she'd cared for her—and her mother.

Perhaps it was the thought of Vicky's mother, Julie, that brought the prickle of tears to the back of Elsie's eyes. She'd asked Elsie if she could stay with Vicky for a few minutes while she went to the cafeteria to buy a favourite brand of ice cream for her daughter. Elsie had promised she wouldn't leave her alone for a second and she wasn't about to now. She had to be able to tell Julie that she'd been here. That everything possible was being done to save her precious child.

It gave her the strength to be able to watch what was happening as Anthony cut through the external sutures and then another layer. He swapped the scalpel for a tool to cut the wires holding the sternum together and his assistant used the pliers to twist and remove the segments of wire.

Seeing the blades of the retractor being slipped into place and a spanner being used to wind it open was enough to make Elsie close her eyes for a moment. She could hear Anthony asking for suction and heard the unit attached to the wall beside the oxygen outlet whirring into action.

'Not much blood loss,' she heard someone close to her say. 'Maybe it's not a tamponade?'

'If it happens fast it takes a lot less blood to cause trouble,' someone else responded, 'Two hundred mils in an adult. But only two mils in a neonate.'

The other doctor who had gowned up was

speaking to Anthony. 'Can you see any active bleeding?'

'No.'

'Have we got a rhythm yet?'

Elsie opened her eyes but she couldn't see the screen of the monitor. She could, however, hear the grim note in Anthony's voice.

'I'm going to try some cardiac massage. Are the internal paddles ready to use for defibrillation?'

'Yes...'

There seemed a moment of hope a short time later when Vicky's heart responded to the massage and began beating but the comments Elsie could hear were concerned with continued bleeding and the danger of hypovolemia. Instructions were being given to make a dash to Theatre, where they might be able to buy enough time to find the source of blood loss and control it.

'Have someone holding the lift doors open,' someone called. 'We'll be ready to move very soon.'

Laura caught Elsie's gaze and she nodded. 'I'll do that.'

It was a relief to get out of the treatment room. She ran to the lifts and pushed the button to summon it, then stood in the doorway to keep the doors open and stop anyone else using it. Seconds later the team emerged from the treatment room—a bed surrounded by people moving swiftly towards the lift. It was obvious that an emergency was in full progress. Anthony was still wearing a blood-stained gown as he strode alongside the bed.

People jumped out of the way, looking shocked. They were still staring after the doors of the lift closed and it began moving up towards the theatre suite. Laura was beside Elsie and they both realised that Vicky's mother was amongst the onlookers. It was obvious that Julie was fearing the worst. Laura spoke quietly to Elsie.

'Stay with her. You're the best person to be looking after her. I'll make sure your other patients are covered for the rest of your shift.'

The ice cream, in its packet, that Julie was holding, slipped from her hand to land on the linoleum floor as Elsie began walking towards her and Elsie knew she had to scrape up the same kind of courage that she'd needed to stay with Vicky during that dramatic resuscitation attempt.

This was going to be even harder. Elsie was a mother herself and she knew the unbearable level of fear that Julie was already experiencing. She had to let her know that everything possible was being done to save Vicky and she couldn't leave Julie alone for a moment while she waited to see if a miracle might be happening upstairs either. Which meant she'd have to be there if the news was as bad as she feared it might be.

At least Elsie knew she could do this as well as anybody else. Better than some, in fact. Because she was a mother herself. Because she understood the challenges and triumphs of raising a child with special needs and just how much of your life and heart they captured.

She also cared very deeply about her patients and their families. This was why she had been so determined to return to the career she'd loved so much—especially her favourite area of paediatrics. This was the downside of the fun and cuddles that came with letting yourself get so involved with these small, vulnerable patients. It was also, arguably, one of the most important aspects of her job.

Elsie walked to Julie, who was still staring at the closed doors of the lift and the lights above it, showing it had reached its destination. She knew that the operating theatres were on that floor. Her voice was no more than a whisper.

'Was that…?'

'It was a sudden collapse.' Elsie put her arm around the younger woman's shoulders to support her because she could feel the shock-wave she was delivering herself. She needed to take her somewhere private and then answer all the questions she could while they waited for an update. 'They're taking Vicky up to Theatre now. They're doing everything they possibly can.'

'I don't understand…' Julie's voice was wooden. 'I was just bringing her an ice cream…'

CHAPTER TWO

THE POPULAR BRANDON HILL PARK was an easy walking distance from Bristol's St Nicholas Children's Hospital in the central city. It was a popular spot with hospital staff who needed a break or wanted to have a picnic lunch outside in nice weather and parents loved it as a place to take their children, thanks to the large sandpit and play area. Paths led up to the landmark of the Cabot Tower at the top of the hill but there were plenty of bench seats to take a rest and admire the view.

Anthony Morgan wasn't planning to sit anywhere. He just needed a bit of exercise and some fresh air. Daylight was about to start fading so it wasn't the best time to be heading into a central city park, but when he'd got to where his car was parked he'd realised he wasn't ready to go home yet. He needed a distraction from the rawness of what had been a very bad day at work.

Something like the noise and activity of that group of teenagers using the sloping paths to practice their skateboarding skills. The children's playground was deserted, which wasn't surprising given the time of day, so there was no distraction there, but he could watch the people who were taking their dogs out after they'd been confined all day. Halfway up the grassy hill, a man was throwing a frisbee for an exuberant collie whose joyous barking as he chased the flying toy towards the trees almost brought a smile to Anthony's face.

He paused for a moment to catch his breath when he reached the tower but was about to turn back and retrace his steps when his attention was caught, seeing someone sitting on one of the seats positioned to have the best view.

A woman.

A woman wearing jeans and long boots. As Anthony got a little closer he could see the silvery streaks in her hair and, even though she had her head bent, he recognised her. And he knew exactly why she was sitting here, alone in this park.

Looking rather like he was feeling himself.

As much as he might have preferred to keep himself to himself, the way he did as much as possible out of work hours, he couldn't simply turn away and leave her here. It wasn't a particularly safe place to be for a woman on her own, for one thing. And he knew too much about her for another.

He knew that her day at work had been as bad—if not possibly even worse—than his. For the same reason, which gave them a connection he couldn't ignore. Not only that, she'd been kind to him when he'd been clumsy enough to spill coffee everywhere the other night. Kind people deserved kindness in return.

He walked towards the bench. 'It's Elsie, isn't it?'

Anthony watched as she used the back of her hand to catch a drip from her nose before looking up at him and those tear-drenched, expressive eyes touched some part of his heart that was usually very well protected.

He took the neatly folded handkerchief from the top pocket of his suit jacket and offered it to her but she shook her head.

'It's okay… I've got a tissue somewhere.'

'Please…'

Anthony pressed the handkerchief into her hands and was rewarded with a shaky smile as she accepted it. The vigorous nose blow that followed made him smile as well.

'Mind if I sit down for a minute?' he asked, even though he was already starting to fold his long legs so that he could sit beside her. 'I think we might both need a bit of company, yes?'

She was still clutching his handkerchief. And then she burst into tears all over again.

Oh, dear Lord, how embarrassing was this?

Elsie Henderson wasn't an inexperienced, newly graduated nurse who had yet to learn how to cope with the more difficult aspects of their chosen career. She was fifty-eight years old, for heaven's sake. A mother. A grandmother. Four decades past being a junior nurse who could be excused for falling apart on the job.

Except she wasn't at work. She'd changed out of her scrubs at the end of one of the most difficult shifts she'd ever experienced but couldn't bring herself to go home straight away. Her grandson, Felix, would have sensed how upset she was and how could she tell him that a little girl, who could so easily have been one of his friends from the support group for spina bifida families, had died today. On top of that, her own daughter, Brie, was about the same age as Julie so it had all been far too close to home, and that had made it even more devastating to have been the last person to hold little Vicky while she was still alive. Elsie would be haunted for ever by that whispery voice telling her that her head was going *'roundy roundy...'*

And now here she was, bawling her eyes out in front of the surgeon she'd been trying to avoid for days. Blowing her nose on the pristine square of soft white cotton with a blue stripe around its neatly hemmed edges. Who used real handkerchiefs these days, anyway? And who ironed them for Anthony Morgan? A housekeeper? His wife?

Oh…no… Elsie screwed her eyes shut. There it was again—that thing she knew about him that he had no idea of. It was easy to push aside, however, because there was something she really needed to ask far more than anything she might think she needed to tell.

'Was it a huge mistake, taking her out of bed like that? I was so careful when I picked her up and it was only for a minute or two.'

Elsie could feel tears gathering again. 'Could it have been enough to start something bleeding?'

'It's looking as if it could have been an arrhythmia rather than a tamponade that caused the arrest.' Anthony sounded weary. As if he'd been going over and over every detail himself in the hours since his small patient had collapsed? 'We came close to losing her that first night after her surgery because of rhythm issues.'

'I remember,' Elsie said. 'That was the night I found you in the staffroom getting a coffee at five a.m.'

Anthony's nod told her that he hadn't forgotten. 'We might end up not getting a definitive answer on what caused Vicky's death, but there are always risks with major surgery like that and one thing I *can* tell you is that it wasn't caused by anything you did. There was no obvious damage to any of the repairs that were done to her heart. And even if she'd still been in the intensive care unit and hooked up to monitors we would have done exactly what we did on the ward and then in Theatre and I doubt very much that it would have made any difference to the outcome.'

It was comforting to hear the reassurance.

Elsie looked up with the intention of thanking Anthony, only to find herself under a steady gaze.

'I remember something else about meeting you the other night.'

To her astonishment, Elsie could feel a bit of warmth colouring her cheeks. She wasn't used to men remembering things about her. It was a little embarrassing to have a man even thinking about her, in fact.

'You told me you were helping raise a grandson with spina bifida.'

'Yes. Felix is six years old. My daughter Brie is a single mum so she's been living with me ever since we knew that there were problems with the pregnancy.'

Anthony's gaze softened. 'Today must have been very hard for you. I'm sorry…'

Elsie nodded. But she could see the lines of stress around his eyes and how weary it made him look. Feeling a bit shy, as if she might be overstepping a boundary, she caught his gaze again. 'For you too,' she said softly.

Anthony didn't say anything but, after a moment's hesitation, he nodded slowly, letting his breath out in a sigh and looking away from her to the view of the city in front of them. Lights were coming on here and there now and it was getting colder. She should be heading home but there was something about that sigh that kept her from moving. She already knew how much this man cared about his patients.

She had seen those lines of weariness in his face before and, okay, it had been after being up all night with Vicky straight after her surgery, but she'd thought at the time that there was something a lot deeper than being overly tired. That he'd looked incredibly sad as well. Lost, even, as he'd stared at a photograph in the newspaper he was holding.

A photograph of his son. A paramedic who'd caught the attention of a journalist by being involved in a mountain rescue. A young man that Elsie knew shared the same surname as this surgeon, but Brie had assured her they weren't related. He'd told her that.

He specifically said he had no family here…

But she'd known there was a connection. Nobody would look like that if it had been a stranger who simply had the same common surname.

'*Do you know him?*' she had asked softly. '*Is he a relative of yours?*'

'*Yeah…*' That single word had carried an

astonishing undertone of pain. *'Jonathon Morgan is my son.'*

How hard would it be to have to tell parents that they'd lost a child, as he'd had to do with Julie and her husband this afternoon, when he had a son himself, even if there was clearly a difficult relationship between father and son? What was it he'd also said that night?

Oh…yes… How could she have forgotten? He'd said he was sure she wouldn't want to hear about his personal life. And then he'd looked away with a wry smile on his face and dismissed the subject with a throwaway comment about how complicated families could be.

And that comment had been haunting her ever since. It was the reason she'd been trying to avoid Anthony Morgan today, when she had her first day shift after her days off. Even now, despite knowing that he was probably as upset as she was about Vicky, she knew she couldn't tell him what he didn't know. That her daughter would probably never forgive her if she did.

'I should get home,' she heard herself saying. 'Brie will be starting to wonder where I am, even though I warned her I was going to be late.'

'It is getting dark.' Anthony followed her example and got to his feet. 'So I can't let you walk back through the park on your own.' He offered her a smile as they began walking. 'Tell me about Felix,' he invited. 'He's a couple of years older than Vicky, you said?'

Elsie blinked. He remembered more than she would have expected of that first conversation, didn't he?

'He's six,' she confirmed. 'And the degree of his spina bifida is much less severe than Vicky's was. He had in utero surgery to close the defect in his spine when Brie was about twenty-five weeks pregnant.'

'Really? I didn't realise that was happening here then.'

'It wasn't. We had to go to Switzerland. It was about then that I decided to give up work to support Brie.'

'You were nursing at St Nick's then?' They were leaving the shadow of the tower behind them as they went downhill. 'I don't remember seeing you around.'

As if he would, Elsie thought. Women started to become a lot less visible in their forties. By the time they hit their fifties they were pretty much part of the background.

'I was working at Central then, but my first

love has always been paediatrics. I had a stint as a general practice nurse too. The hours worked a lot better for me when Brie was at primary school and I was a single mum. It's been a recent thing to go back to nursing but I needed something else in my life and… I'm loving it…' Elsie's voice suddenly wobbled. 'Apart from today…'

'There are always bad days,' Anthony said. 'But, fortunately, they're outweighed by the good ones.' She could hear a smile in his voice. 'And we need nurses like you, Elsie. People that understand what the parents, as much as their children, are going through.'

They walked in silence for a minute or two and then they were out of the gates to the park and on the road leading back to St Nick's.

'How are you getting home?' Anthony asked as they waited for the lights to change and let them cross a busy junction with a group of shops on the other side of the main road. 'Can I offer you a lift?'

Elsie shook her head. 'I have my car at work.'

'And your daughter will be at home when you get there? And Felix?'

'It will be exactly what I need,' she confessed. 'I just needed to get a good cry out of the way before I got there.' She bit her lip, knowing that she was treading on personal ground. 'I hope you've got some company at home too?'

Anthony gave her an odd look. 'I lost my family a very long time ago,' he said quietly.

Elsie knew she shouldn't take an even bigger leap into that personal space but she couldn't fight the urge. Not when she was this emotionally exhausted and couldn't bear the thought that this man who'd been kind enough to offer her comfort—not to mention his hanky—despite being so upset himself, would be going home to an empty house.

'But…' she snatched a breath '…you have a son… Jonno…'

The lights changed and people nearby walked away but Anthony was staring at Elsie and she couldn't move.

'How on earth did you know that?' he asked.

'You told me. When you saw the photograph of him in the paper.'

'But I told you that his name was Jonathon. How did you know Jonno has always been my son's nickname?'

It was too late to stop now. Apparently that step into this personal space was actually the top of a slippery slope that was even steeper than the hill they'd just come down together. And the emotional consequences after such a traumatic day had done something more than exhaust Elsie. They'd removed any barriers she'd had about telling Anthony what she knew. It was suddenly blindingly clear that he had the right to know, and at the end of a day like this perhaps he *needed* to know.

'My daughter knew him,' she heard herself saying calmly. 'She met him just before he went overseas a while back. Before…she knew she was pregnant…'

Their chance to cross the road on this cycle had gone but Anthony didn't seem to have noticed. His gaze was locked on Elsie's. He might be as tired as she was but that wasn't stopping his brain from working with impressive speed.

'Are you saying…that my son is the father of your grandson?'

Elsie took a deep breath. 'Yes,' she said.

Anthony gave his head a tiny shake. 'One of the last things he said to me was that he was never going to get married. Or have children. That the last thing he would ever do would be to live the kind of lie I'd been living. Unless…' He was frowning now. 'Unless it was history repeating itself and it was an accident…?'

'It was.' Elsie nodded. 'Brie was on the pill but she got sick…'

The expression on Anthony's face was unreadable now. Stunned, even. 'But that means…'

'Yes.' Elsie kept holding his gaze. 'Felix is your grandson too.'

There were people gathering beside them to wait for the next window of time to cross the road but Elsie didn't move an inch. She could see the moment that the implications of what she was telling him registered with Anthony. She was getting a glimpse of a part of this man that she instinctively knew was usually kept very private.

Just for a heartbeat she could see the flare of something that looked like longing in his eyes, but then he blinked and it was gone.

'Jonno's not really my son,' he said. 'Not biologically. I just…thought he was until he did a DNA test when he was about eighteen.'

Oh…wow… No wonder she had sensed a whole world of pain beneath his words when he'd seen that picture of his son in the newspaper. It seemed very unfair that a man that Elsie already knew to be kind and caring might have been hurt badly enough to feel the need to deny something that was clearly so important to him.

'You raised him,' she said quietly. 'You loved him. You're his dad and that makes him your son as far as I'm concerned.' She was ignoring the curious glances of strangers moving past them to cross the road as the traffic waited. 'And that also makes Felix your grandson.'

Maybe it was a trick of the light, with darkness falling around them and the traffic light beside them changing colour, but Elsie was almost sure she could see tears in Anthony's eyes now and that pulled her heartstrings so hard she could feel tears of her own gathering again. Without thinking, she put her hand on Anthony's arm, as if she needed to confirm the connection they had. She also wasn't really thinking when she opened her mouth to speak again.

'Would you like to meet him?' she asked.

CHAPTER THREE

IT TURNED OUT to be remarkably easy.

As if it had been meant to happen?

All it took was for Elsie to suggest a new park to go to on the way home from school. One that had a big sandpit and a climbing frame and a tall tower on top of a hill.

'It's near where Nana works,' she told Felix. 'At your hospital.'

'Do I have to go to hostible again?' Felix had always had trouble with the pronunciation of the institution he'd spent too much time in already in his six years.

'No.' Elsie gave him a cuddle. 'It's just that I went there the other day and it was so nice I thought you might like to see the tower. It might be nice for Dennis to have a new place to walk too, don't you think?'

And how natural did it seem when Nana came across a friend of hers from work who was taking a break that afternoon and just happened to be walking near the play area when they got there?

'I'm pleased to meet you, Felix.' Anthony crouched in front of the small wheelchair so he wasn't towering over the small boy. 'My name's Anthony. And who's this?' He reached out to scratch the ears of the small woolly dog sitting by the chair's footplate.

'Dennis,' Felix told him. 'We've come here to have a walk and go to the playground.' He beamed at Anthony. 'There's a tower here too. On top of the hill. It's really tall.'

'It's an awesome tower.' Anthony returned the smile, the way everybody automatically did when Felix smiled at them, but this time Elsie's heart melted a lot more than usual. Because this man was another grandparent for Felix and she could remember that astonishing joy when she'd held him in her arms for the first time, knowing that he was the child of her child, which made him a part of her own heart. Was Anthony feeling that unique kind of love already? His smile suggested that he was because Elsie had never seen him smile like that before.

And it was a lovely smile. Felix seemed to be basking in it.

'I want to climb it,' Felix confided to Anthony. 'But Nana said maybe not today because my legs might get too tired. That's why we brought my chair. I *can* walk, you know. Would you like to see me climb and go down the slide?'

'I would indeed.'

'You sit there,' Felix commanded, pointing to a bench seat. 'With Nana.' He was climbing out of his wheelchair. 'And Dennis,' he added as an afterthought. 'Because he might think he's at the beach and dig holes in the sand.'

So Elsie and Anthony sat on the bench. Dennis sat beside Elsie's feet and watched the squirrels, who darted closer in the hope of being offered something to eat, but the adults were watching Felix as he made a beeline towards the climbing frame.

'Is he okay to do that on his own?' Anthony asked.

Elsie nodded. 'He'll be careful. And it's got handrails and those logs for steps on the ramp. He'd hate me to be hovering over him like a helicopter nana, especially when he's arranged a captive audience.'

'He's a happy wee chap.' Anthony seemed to be watching Felix carefully. 'And confi-

dent. It doesn't look that easy for him, walking through the sand, but he's not letting it
slow him down.' He smiled. 'He reminds me
so much of Jonno at that age, which is a bit
odd.'

'Well… I had another look at that photograph of Jonno in the paper.' Elsie gave Anthony a quick, shy glance. 'I cut it out to keep
for Felix—not that he knows about his father
yet. Jonno doesn't know about Felix either,
but that's a whole different story.' She shook
her head. 'What I was going to say is that I
thought you and Jonno look remarkably alike,
so it's not surprising that Felix reminds you
of your son.'

Anthony shrugged. 'Maybe it's the colouring. Dark hair, dark eyes… I'd always thought
he looked far more like me than his mother,
but there you go… DNA doesn't lie. And I'd
always known it was a possibility.'

Elsie blinked. 'Really?' She turned to
check on Felix as he negotiated the ramp of
the climbing frame. 'How?'

Anthony was quiet for a moment and then
she heard him take a deep breath. 'I guess
people don't talk about it so much these days.'
He let the breath out in a sigh. 'Maybe it's

only me that feels as if the scandal is a permanent shadow over my life.'

'I don't listen to gossip,' Elsie told him. She offered him a smile. 'And you don't have to tell me about it. As far as I'm concerned you're Felix's grandpa and that's all that matters.'

'Except...it isn't, is it?' Anthony's words were quiet. 'It matters that Jonno doesn't know he's a father, doesn't it?'

Elsie nodded. And then she echoed Anthony's sigh. 'I've made my feelings very clear about that to Brie—my daughter—but she says she's got to find the right moment.' She waved at Felix, who'd reached the top of the ramp. 'I should tell you that she did do her best to contact him as soon as she knew she was pregnant but he was long gone. Off to the Himalayas and he never responded to her on social media. And then she found out that her baby had spina bifida and...well... life changed for both of us. Trying to track down someone Brie had only ever been with once didn't seem that important. Especially when nobody knew where he was exactly.'

'He's good at flying under the radar.' Anthony nodded. 'Even when he was still in the UK, I had trouble trying to stay in touch.'

'He's not planning to stay here for long either. Brie says he's going to sell the apartment he owns and then he'll be gone again. For good, this time.'

'Oh…' The syllable was drawn out. As if Anthony had expected little else? Elsie wasn't about to ask, but she had to admit she was curious about what could have caused such a breakdown in the relationship between a father and son. Surely it wasn't only because it was lacking a biological link?

'Brie's worried about how it might affect Felix if he discovers he has a daddy who then walks out on him and disappears, but I've said that he has the right to know. And that maybe he'll change his mind about going somewhere else when he knows he has a son.' But Elsie was frowning now. 'Have you not heard anything from him since he left? In nearly seven *years*?'

'Longer than that. He pretty much turned his back on me after his mother's death. He blamed me for the accident. For the whole scandal, in fact.'

There was that word again and it just didn't fit with this man who seemed as dignified as the pinstriped suit he was wearing. As caring as the smile he'd given to Felix had suggested? Maybe Elsie's confusion was written all over her face because Anthony made a wry face.

'You should know about it,' he said. 'It's part of what makes this situation so very complicated.'

The shriek of glee from the small boy as he went down the slide was anything but complicated. Felix was living in the moment and having a great time.

'Did you see me, Nana? I went down the slide by myself.'

'I *did* see you, darling. It looked like great fun.'

'I'm going to do it again.' Felix climbed off the slide but found himself behind another child about to climb the ramp. 'When it's my turn...' He was grinning at a girl who was standing behind him now. 'It's the bestest slide, isn't it? What's your name...?'

It wasn't just the colour of his hair or eyes that was reminding Anthony of the son he'd raised.

It was that *charm*...

He was under its spell already himself— even more than the little girl with pigtails who was watching with open admiration as Felix climbed the ramp again.

'Jonno's mother was a nurse at St Nick's,' he told Elsie, his voice without expression. 'It could be a case of history repeating itself with Jonno, but on my first date with Julia…' he cleared his throat delicately '…we got a little carried away. We went out a few more times over the next month or so and then she told me she was pregnant.' He was silent for a long moment. 'Long story short, we got married. Jonno was born and he was the best thing that had ever happened to me and I did think we could make it work, but I was wrong. I found out Julia was having an affair before he was even a year old, and it was only the first of many.'

'Oh, my goodness…' Elsie sounded horrified. 'But you stayed married to her?'

'We lived in the same house.' Anthony nodded. 'But it was never a real marriage. She didn't need the money—she was wealthy in her own right—but she wanted to be a surgeon's wife and the Morgan name has been well known in certain circles in Bristol for generations. It can open doors no amount of money could have done.' He paused to take a slow breath. 'She would have taken Jonno away from me if I hadn't agreed. I would never have seen him again. Not that I was allowed too much time with him, mind you. He got sent to boarding school at a young age and if she thought he was getting too attached to me when we did get time together, she'd whisk him away on holiday. Somewhere tropical usually, with her latest lover in tow.'

Elsie was silent but he could feel her shock that he would have put up with the situation and, looking back, he felt ashamed. She didn't say anything. She seemed to be focused on Felix, who'd given up on the slide. He was playing in the sand with his new friend with the pigtails. It looked as if they were making roads and using small sticks and stones as cars.

'I spent more and more time at work,' he admitted quietly. 'I didn't want to break up Jonno's family when he was young and have him turned against me but it happened anyway. When Julia was killed in the car accident, it became public knowledge that she was in the car with a man who wasn't her husband and it was big news because he ran one of the biggest national charities and people had all thought he was completely trustworthy. And then it all came out. The string of affairs, including other high-profile men. The discreet apartment she owned that she used as her 'love nest'. The public face she'd maintained in her involvement with all sorts of charities and the glamorous fundraising events she loved. The complete farce of her marriage...'

He took a breath but it was too swift to give Elsie the chance to make any comment. He hadn't got to the part that she probably needed to know.

'Jonno blamed me. He'd adored his mother and had no idea what was really going on. With all the wisdom of a fifteen-year-old, he decided that if I'd been a better husband she wouldn't have gone looking for anyone else. And if I'd been a better father I would have spent more time with him. He was grieving. And he was very angry. He went back to boarding school and when the holidays rolled around there were always friends that invited him to stay. Or go on adventures. He got into skiing in a big way. Rock climbing. Scuba diving. Any sport that created enough adrenaline to distract him, I guess. I encouraged it even because I thought he'd get past it as he grew up a little more, but he refused to ever discuss it. When he was eighteen he inherited the apartment and rather a lot of money from his mother's estate and he moved out. That was when he did the DNA test I told you about.' Anthony's words trailed into silence. He'd said more than enough.

Too much, perhaps? Did Elsie see him as most people had back then—including his son—as being weak? A total failure as a husband and a father? The reason his mother had been unfaithful and, by extension, the cause of her death?

Felix had given up on the game in the sand and he was coming towards them, limping a little.

'I'm hungry, Nana,' he announced.

'So are those squirrels,' Elsie said. 'We must remember to bring them something to eat next time we come.'

Next time? Anthony wanted to catch her gaze in case that was a subtle invitation for them to do this again. He rather hoped it was, but Elsie was making sure Felix was comfortable in his wheelchair.

'I'm a bit hungry myself, come to think about it,' she said. 'How 'bout we go to one of those cafés near where we parked the car and have a treat for afternoon tea? That way, we can put Dennis in the car to wait for us.'

'Can I have a sausage roll?'

'I'm sure they'll have sausage rolls.' Elsie turned to Anthony and her smile suggested that his interpretation of an unspoken invitation to meet again was not wrong. It also told him that she didn't think any less of him after hearing his story. If anything, her smile was even warmer than he'd seen before.

Warm enough to light up tiny golden speckles in those brown eyes that were an unusual colour that made him think of milk chocolate. Or had those flecks been there all along and he just hadn't taken any notice? Like he hadn't noticed that there were parts of Elsie's hair that weren't grey and it was that same shade of brown as her eyes? There were crinkles around her eyes as well that told him she smiled a lot.

Who wouldn't with the joy that her adorable grandson would bring into her life?

Their adorable grandson?

'Come with us,' she invited. 'Do you like sausage rolls too?'

Something was squeezing in Anthony's chest, hard enough to make it hard to take a breath.

'They're my absolute favourite,' he lied.

And then he told the truth. 'I'd love to come with you.'

The sausage rolls were hot and savoury and they even had tomato sauce in squeezy plastic tomatoes, which Felix highly approved of.

'It's got a green stalk, just like a *real* tomato.' His tone was awed.

Elsie and Anthony shared a glance. 'I wonder how much of any *real* tomatoes are inside,' she said. The way Anthony quirked his eyebrow made her realise he wasn't about to let anything like nutritional guidelines undermine the sheer pleasure Felix was getting from this treat and she liked that. She could feel the connection growing between this man and his grandson. Between all three of them, in fact, and she liked that too.

She liked it a lot.

The café was not too busy. Two women were carrying plates with wedges of delicious-looking chocolate cake to a nearby table and a man and woman were waiting near the coffee machine having placed a takeaway order. The table closest to the window was ready to be cleared of its crockery but the young woman behind the counter was busy making the coffees. Nobody could have had the slightest idea of what was about to hap-

pen in this small café as Elsie tried to collect
some of the flaky pastry crumbs that were
landing all over Felix's jumper.

It took a moment for Elsie to even process what was happening when the huge glass
window shattered with such a loud bang and
the whole frontage of the café seemed to be
caving in. Both she and Anthony instinctively
moved to try and shelter Felix. Elsie was closest and she put her hands on the back of the
wheelchair and hunched her body to create a
human wall in front of her precious grandson.
Then she felt Anthony's arm coming around
her shoulders. He was trying to protect both
of them. From what? A bomb going off?

The thought was so horrific Elsie twisted to
try and see and her gaze caught on Anthony's.

'Are you okay?' he asked. 'And Felix?'

'I think so…' Elsie was still stunned.
'Felix? Are you okay, darling?'

Felix nodded. He was trying to peer past
his grandmother. 'Look…' He pointed his finger. 'There's a *car…inside…*'

Sure enough, there was a car that had
crashed through the plate glass window, de-
molishing the table that hadn't been cleared
so there was now a lot of broken crockery
amongst a deep layer of shattered glass on

the floor. The man who'd been waiting for his coffee order was holding his arm and had blood dripping from his hand. The two women had completely forgotten about their cake and were staring in shock. A man in a chef's apron came rushing out from the back with a tea towel draped over his shoulder.

'I've called the police,' he shouted. 'And an ambulance. Don't move yet. There's glass everywhere.'

'I'm a doctor.' Anthony stood up. He was moving towards the car.

Elsie could see a dazed-looking elderly man in the driver's seat who appeared to be conscious. She saw the way Anthony scanned the whole scene. He needed to get to the car as fast as possible because the engine was still revving. If the driver put his foot on the accelerator could it come any further inside? Elsie moved to pull Felix's wheelchair further back, wondering if there was a back door in the kitchen that they might be able to escape through.

The flying glass hadn't reached the two women but it had clearly caught the man with the bleeding arm, who was the first person Anthony got to.

'I pulled the glass out,' the man said. 'But it's bleeding too much, isn't it?'

Anthony turned to the chef. 'Can you fold that tea towel to make a pad? That cut needs pressure on it to stop the bleeding. I need to check on the driver. And it might be a good idea if you can all move back a little in case the car gets past whatever's obstructing it.'

Suddenly, Elsie realised that Anthony might be putting himself in danger going anywhere near the car and her own level of alarm increased markedly. What if the car moved and hit him? Or it caught fire? What if the elderly driver had a head injury and became aggressive? Part of her wanted to go and help Anthony but an even bigger part was keeping her where she was, to protect Felix. At least it wasn't going to be long before the experts in dealing with emergencies like this arrived on scene. Amazingly, Elsie could already hear an approaching siren outside.

She backed Felix into what seemed to be a safe corner and decided it was definitely better to stay where they were for the moment. It didn't look as though her first aid skills were going to be needed either, because Anthony seemed to have things under control already. He'd managed to open the driver's door of the car, turn the engine off and he was now crouched beside the elderly man, asking him questions. She saw the man shaking his head as if he had no idea of what was going on and was finding it all very alarming.

There wasn't much left of the front door to the café but that was where Elsie saw the first emergency service personnel arriving only moments later and for a moment she felt as stunned as the elderly driver seemed to be. How on earth could this be happening? It was Felix who knew exactly what was going on.

'*Mumma!*' he shouted. 'Look, Nana…it's *Mumma.*'

Her daughter, Brie, who was a recently qualified paramedic was part of the team responding to this emergency and being found out in what had been supposed to be a secret rendezvous was the last thing Elsie would have wanted to happen. Not that Brie had any idea of what she'd done yet but she was going to find out any minute because, thanks to that picture in the newspaper that had been the catalyst for this meeting in the first place, Elsie had recognised the uniformed man who'd walked in with Brie as being Jonathon Morgan.

Felix's father.

Anthony's son.

It was a ticking emotional time bomb but the only thing Brie was worried about so far was that her son had been part of a traumatic incident. She veered away from Jonno and rushed towards the corner where Elsie and Felix were.

'Mum...what on earth are you doing here? Are you hurt?' Brie dropped to crouch in front of the wheelchair. 'Felix? Are you okay, darling?'

Felix had already climbed out of his wheelchair as he saw his mother coming towards them so he was ready to throw his arms around her neck and be gathered up into a comforting cuddle.

'The car came through the window, Mumma,' he told her excitedly.

'We came to Brandon Hill Park for a walk after school,' Elsie added hurriedly, although the plan of pretending they'd met Anthony Morgan by coincidence was seeming completely unfeasible now. 'It's got a nice playground. Felix got hungry so we thought we'd treat ourselves to afternoon tea.'

'I had a sausage roll, Mumma. And look... the tomato sauce is in a *real* tomato...'

But, having been reassured that both Felix

and her mother were unhurt, Brie wasn't listening. She had turned to scan the area and see where she needed to be to be doing her job. Another paramedic was entering the café, carrying more equipment, but it was Jonno that caught both Elsie and Brie's immediate attention.

Elsie knew why Jonno looked so shocked when Anthony stood up from where he'd been crouched beside the driver, with only his back visible, and turned to face Jonno. This was the first time in so many years that father and son had even seen each other, let alone be standing with only a matter of inches between them.

In that moment, Anthony must have realised that there was going to be a price for Elsie to pay for having arranged their meeting because his gaze flew to meet hers and, even from this distance, she could see understanding, if not an apology, being offered. She could also hear the icy anger in Jonno's voice in the first, fierce words he said to his father.

'What the *hell* is going on here?'

Brie was hurriedly putting Felix back into his wheelchair. The other paramedic was moving in to help Jonno and Anthony was stepping back.

'What *is* going on, Mum?' Brie demanded. 'Who is that man? Someone said he's a doctor, so what's so wrong about him helping the driver of that car?'

'Nothing,' Elsie confirmed. 'He *is* a doctor. He's Anthony Morgan. He's also Jonno's father,' she added, quietly enough not to distract Felix from his fascinated attention on what was happening near the car. 'He…um… wanted to meet his grandson.'

She could see the shock of Brie realising what had been going on. The shock of feeling completely betrayed was only a heartbeat later and Elsie's heart sank like a stone. She'd known she was taking a risk but she'd thought it would all come right with a bit of time. After Brie had done what should have been done already and told Jonno that he was Felix's father?

The choice of when that happened had just been taken away from her, hadn't it?

'How *could* you?' Brie's tone was like a physical blow. 'Take Felix home, please.'

'But…'

'*Now*…' Brie ignored her mother and touched her son's head. 'I'll see you soon, but I've got work I have to do right now.' She walked away, towards the man with the bloodstained tea towel. 'Can I see your arm?' Elsie heard her ask. 'How did your injury happen?'

Anthony was beside them again.

'I'm so sorry,' Elsie said. 'We shouldn't have come here.'

'I'm glad we did,' Anthony said calmly. 'But I do think it's time we left. Let me help you get Felix back to your car.'

Firemen helped lift the wheelchair over the debris and onto the footpath outside. A police officer took their details and told them that they would be contacted soon to make a statement about what they'd witnessed. Someone lifted the bright yellow and black tape that was keeping spectators away from an emergency scene and, only a few minutes later, Anthony was helping Elsie lift Felix into his car seat and fold the wheelchair to go in the back of her hatchback.

'What about the man?' Felix asked when Anthony leaned down to say goodbye.

'What man?' It was Elsie who answered. Quickly, in case it somehow slipped out that Felix had just seen the father he didn't know he had.

'The man in the car? Was he dead?'

'No, no…' It was Anthony who provided

instant reassurance. 'He wasn't really hurt at all because he was wearing his seat belt and the airbag in the car protected him as well. He was a bit confused about what had happened and I think that was because he'd put his foot on the wrong pedal and gone faster instead of stopping.' He was smiling at Felix. 'But don't you worry. Nothing really bad happened and it's all going to be okay.'

His smile faded as he straightened to catch Elsie's gaze, however.

They both knew that something had happened. Something that had nothing to do with a confused elderly man who'd put his foot on the wrong pedal.

Something that was going to change the lives of everybody involved.

And…it might not turn out to be okay at all…

CHAPTER FOUR

'ARJUN, PUT THAT down right now! The nurse wants to take your temperature.'

The eight-year-old boy made a frustrated sound but obeyed his mother and put his tablet down reluctantly. 'But I'll miss my frog's heart dividing, Mummy. It's going to have three chambers now.'

'You know this game off by heart, Arjun.' His mother, Shayana, was shaking her head but her smile was proud.

'I've got four chambers in my heart, haven't I, Elsie?'

'You certainly have.' Elsie looked down at the screen as she put the tip of the tympanic thermometer in Arjun's ear and pressed the button. 'That looks like a great game. I bet my grandson Felix would absolutely love it.'

'I can dissect my frog. I'll show you.'

But Elsie caught his arm. 'In a minute,

sweetheart. Your doctor's coming to see you any time now and if I haven't done your blood pressure and heart rate and everything else, he'll growl at me.'

'Will he?' Arjun's face lit up in a smile. 'Mummy growls at me a lot.'

'I do not,' Shayana protested. 'He's such a good boy,' she told Elsie. 'How could I growl at him a lot?'

Elsie smiled as she fitted her stethoscope to her ears. 'See how quiet you can be for just a bit, Arjun. I need to be able to listen so I can hear your blood pressure.' She could almost feel the little boy bursting with impatience as she inflated the cuff around his arm and then let it down slowly.

'Can you really hear my blood?' he demanded as soon as she lifted the disc of the stethoscope from his arm. 'What sort of noise does it make?'

'Dub-dub-dub…' Elsie told him. 'It's part of the same noise your heart makes, which is lub-dub, lub-dub, lub-dub…'

Arjun laughed and mimicked the sound, bouncing up and down on his bed at the same time, but Elsie could see his mother wiping tears from her eyes.

'You can play your game again now,' she

told Arjun. Then she reached for the chart on the end of his bed to record her observations and spoke quietly to Shayana. 'Are you okay?'

She nodded. 'I'm just so happy,' she whispered. 'It was such a big operation and it was only last week and look at him now...'

'Come and see,' Arjun commanded. 'I'm going to start the dissection of my frog now.'

'A dissection? Goodness me, what's going on in here?'

They all turned to see Arjun's surgeon come into the room with one of his registrars and what looked to be some medical students who were observing his ward round this morning. Anthony Morgan's smile was most likely the kind he gave all his small patients and their mothers but, because Elsie was standing beside Shayana, she got the full benefit as well and her day instantly got a little brighter.

Hurriedly, she began filling in the empty spaces on Arjun's chart with the latest recordings but Anthony didn't need it yet. He was sitting on the side of the bed looking at the screen of the tablet with great interest.

Arjun wasn't at all bothered by how many people had just come into his room. He was focused on his surgeon. 'So I pin him like this.' Arjun tapped the screen on several points. 'And then I can cut his skin and fold it back and see all his organs. See?'

'Wow…' Anthony looked suitably impressed. 'I think you'll be doing my job in no time flat. Has your frog got a heart?'

'Of course. I'll find it for you. I can even take it out and put it on the tray.'

'You do that while we talk about you for a minute, okay? These visitors are learning to be doctors and someone like you is very interesting for them to know about.'

Arjun nodded absentmindedly. He was busy with the game that was directing which organs he needed to find first.

'Arjun is just over a week post-op now after coronary artery bypass graft surgery to repair a giant coronary artery aneurysm,' Anthony told the students. 'And, as you can see, he's doing very well.' He caught Elsie's gaze. 'Are you happy with him this morning?'

'I am,' she responded. 'All his vital sign recordings are within normal parameters. There are no issues with his cardiac rhythm or his fluid balance, there's no sign of infection in his wound and he hasn't needed any pain relief except for the paracetamol.'

'I'll let my registrar fill you in on Arjun's past medical history,' Anthony said to the students. 'I'm just going to have a quick read of the notes made since I saw him yesterday.' He stepped closer to Elsie.

'Okay…' His registrar, Ruth, stepped to the other side, nearer the students. 'So Arjun got Kawasaki disease when he was five months old and, despite aggressive therapy, he had an acute infarct three weeks later. He was in hospital for nearly three months.'

Arjun was completely engrossed in his game but his mother was listening to the recap. 'That was such a terrible time for the whole family,' she whispered.

'It must have been,' Elsie sympathised. Anthony flashed a glance at her, looking up from the notes. He knew she wasn't having the best time herself right now, with her own family. He'd been checking in when they found a quiet moment on his ward visits and, to be honest, it had been a relief to have somebody to talk to about what was going on in her private life so Elsie knew she'd probably told him more than he actually wanted to know.

Brie was still absolutely furious with her for having engineered that meeting between Anthony and his grandson. Mother and daughter were barely talking to each other right now and Brie had even made a comment about it being ridiculous to be her age and still living with her parent and maybe it was time she started looking for her own home.

'So Arjun was carefully monitored by Cardiology and the cardiothoracic surgical teams throughout his childhood but CABG could be postponed until his arteries were larger because he was getting a good blood supply from collateral vessels.' Ruth didn't have to look at their patient's notes. She had done her homework well. 'The latest round of tests showed extensive ischaemia, however,' she continued. 'We found a complete occlusion of his left anterior descending artery and ST depression on a ECG treadmill test so we decided it was time for the surgery. Are you all familiar with the process of coronary artery grafting?'

The students all nodded. 'What vessel was used for the graft and how many vessels were grafted?' one asked.

'Two vessels grafted.' Anthony rejoined the conversation. 'And current practice is to use internal thoracic arteries as conduits for coronary bypass grafting in children with Kawasaki disease. They show significantly better results in long-term functionality.' He glanced up at the clock. 'How 'bout you talk about this more with these guys on your way upstairs, Ruth? I'll see you up there shortly, but it could take a while to get everybody sorted for their Theatre observation session. You could give them a bit of a tour of the Theatre suite if you have time.'

The rattle of the food trolley delivering lunch could be heard as the students followed Ruth into the corridor. Anthony hooked the chart back on the bed and smiled at Arjun.

'I can hear your lunch arriving. Can I have a quick look at your zipper before it gets here?'

Arjun grinned and unbuttoned his pyjama top to show off the sutures in the middle of his chest beneath the clear plastic dressing. Again, just for a heartbeat, Anthony Morgan's gaze caught Elsie's and she knew they were both thinking of the same thing.

Vicky…

And maybe that was why, when Anthony had completed a swift check of Arjun's progress and moved aside to let his mother bring in the lunch tray, he smiled at Elsie.

'Got time for a coffee? There's another patient I'd like to talk to you about.'

'Go,' Shayana said to Elsie. 'I can give Arjun his lunch. You didn't even get morning tea, I don't think.'

'Are you sure you've got time?' Elsie asked as she followed Anthony into the corridor. 'There are some eager students waiting for you to demonstrate your skills upstairs.'

'It's their first time anywhere near a theatre. They'll be so excited, it'll take ages to get them kitted out. My patient isn't even due to leave the ward for at least half an hour. And I could really use a coffee.'

'Me too. Shayana's right, it's been so busy I haven't even sat down for five minutes yet.'

Moments later, they were both sitting in the same armchairs they had used the night they'd first met. The pile of folded newspaper on the table looked the same. The coffee tasted exactly the same. What was very different, however, was how comfortable they were with each other, even after the tension of what had happened in the café that day. Maybe it was actually because of it? There was no hesitation on Elsie's part to ask a personal question today when they found they had the staffroom to themselves.

'Has Jonno been in touch with you yet?'

Anthony shook his head. 'I don't really expect him to be,' he admitted. 'He's got a lot on his plate, hasn't he? How has he taken the news that he's a father, do you know?'

'Brie's still not really talking to me,' Elsie told him. 'But I do know that he's spent some time with Felix. He went to a session at Riding for the Disabled and I think he's going to a music and movement class with them this week. I can't ask Brie. I've already interfered too much.' She sipped her coffee and then sighed. 'It's all a bit miserable, to be honest. I get the feeling that she's got some pretty deep feelings for Jonno but I doubt very much that he feels the same way. He's a bit of a lone wolf, isn't he?'

Anthony made a sympathetic sound. 'I can't imagine he's finding any of this easy. Relationships can be so very complicated, can't they?'

Elsie's smile was wry. 'Sometimes I'm rather thankful I'm single.'

'Me too.'

'Really?' Elsie blinked. She'd certainly got the impression that Anthony lived alone, but that didn't necessarily mean he didn't have a partner.

'Really,' Anthony said firmly. 'Once was more than enough for me. Marriage was certainly nothing like I hoped it would be.' He lifted an eyebrow. 'Were you a single mother by choice?'

'Oh, no…my husband died just before Brie was born.'

'I'm sorry to hear that.'

'I was lucky that looking after my baby got me through the worst thing that had ever happened to me. It might have only been a short marriage but it was perfect.'

Anthony drained his coffee mug and got to his feet. 'You were lucky to have had that,' he murmured. He lifted an eyebrow before he turned. 'I'm surprised someone hasn't come along and swept you off your feet since, though.'

Elsie laughed. 'I'm way past any nonsense like that.'

Anthony was smiling as well. 'It's rather nice, isn't it?'

'What? Being single?'

'Being past all that angst.'

'Yes. I feel rather sorry for Jonno at the moment.'

The glance they shared was one of mutual agreement—that it was a relief not to have to deal with the emotional upsets that romantic relationships could bring—but it was a fleeting moment of connection as a nurse poked her head around the door.

'Ah…someone said you might be in here, Mr Morgan. You wouldn't have a minute to talk to Penelope's mum, would you? She's got herself in a bit of a state about her upcoming surgery.'

'No problem. I'll be right there.' Anthony picked up his empty mug. 'Have you met Penny? Three-year-old with hypoplastic left heart syndrome? She's in for a cardiac catheter before her Fontan procedure later this week. It's not as risky as the first operation she had as a newborn but it's still a pretty big deal. I'm not surprised her mum's finding it difficult.'

Elsie held out her hand to take Anthony's mug. 'I can rinse that. You go. Families are our patients too, aren't they? Oh…was Penny the other patient you wanted to talk to me about?'

'No…' Anthony's smile was a little embarrassed. 'That was just an excuse to have a chat.' He turned to leave but then turned back. 'Don't feel too sorry for Jonno,' he said quietly. 'The timing might not have been the best but he needed to know and I'm sure Brie will understand that eventually. And please don't be sorry that you let me meet Felix. I'm really hoping that we can do that again when things settle down a little.'

Elsie rinsed the mugs and slotted them into the dishwasher. She'd been completely honest when she'd told Anthony she was past even thinking about bumping into her soulmate and being swept off her feet to fall hopelessly in love. So why did it feel as if her heart was beating a little faster than normal right now?

Or that being told he'd invented a reason to have a chat with her was giving her an odd curl of pleasure?

That the thought of spending time with him again made that rather pleasant sensation even more noticeable?

And that the fact that he was single had suddenly become far more significant than it had any right to be?

A Fontan procedure was the third major surgery in the series for children who had been born with only one ventricle instead of two, which meant that the way the blood circulated had to be drastically altered if the baby was going to survive. The initial, and most risky, operation could take six to eight hours and usually happened in the first week of life. A second surgery happened at around six months of age and was an intermediary stage before the third, Fontan procedure, that created a way for deoxygenated blood to bypass the heart completely and go straight to the lungs, which decreased the workload in a single ventricle and could dramatically improve the quality of life for the child.

Anthony Morgan was a very well-respected, experienced cardiac surgeon across the entire spectrum of congenital, paediatric and adult cardiac surgery and the Fontan procedure was one of his favourites. He'd been part of the lives of these children since they were born and had a vital role in supporting their families. It was a long and complex enough surgery to shrink the world down to purely what was happening within the four walls of an operating theatre and that had always been the place Anthony felt most at home in. His happy place, where anything personal was irrelevant and he could focus purely on the job at hand—a job he knew he was good at which made him confident and calm, despite any emotional involvement with his patients and how invested he was in getting a successful result.

Oh, things could get tense, of course. There

were often complications to manage during and after the surgery where a major blood vessel got disconnected from the heart and joined to the pulmonary artery, with a connection created that would control the flow of blood to the lungs until the body adjusted to the new anatomy. Occasionally a battle was lost, along with a young life, and that was deeply upsetting.

Anthony had never had a post-op disruption quite like the one he got today, however, when he finally turned his phone back on after seeing Penny transferred from Recovery to the PICU, to find a voicemail waiting for him.

One that had been left a few hours ago now.

Hearing his son's voice on the recording was enough to make him catch his breath. Hearing a siren in the background, along with Jonno's words, made it impossible to let it go.

'Hi, Dad. It's Jonno. The operator put me through to your phone when she found out you were in Theatre. I'm on my way to St Nick's with Felix. He's had a seizure. He's still having one, actually. We've got him intubated to protect his airway.' There was a long moment's silence and Anthony could almost feel the struggle his son was having to find the words to say something else. And perhaps he gave up.

'… I just thought you should know…'

Sitting beside her precious grandson, who had a ventilator breathing for him as he lay in the intensive care unit waiting for decisions to be made in the next stage of his treatment, made Elsie Henderson feel like this had been one of the longest ever days in her life and it wasn't even lunchtime yet.

That dreadful call from Brie to tell her they were on the way in to the hospital had been hours ago now but it felt a lot longer. Being in here alone while Brie and Jonno were talking to Felix's neurosurgeon had made the minutes drag past even more slowly, especially when it seemed that Brie had been gone for too long. Her daughter's face was so pale when she returned that Elsie felt as if her heart was breaking. She was holding Felix's hand with one of hers and she stretched the other towards her daughter to draw her closer.

'We've signed the consent forms,' Brie told her. 'They'll be getting Felix ready any time now to go up to Theatre. They have to take the shunt that drains the cerebral spinal fluid out so they can treat the infection that's causing all the problems.'

Elsie nodded. And swallowed hard. 'Where's Jonno?'

'In the relatives' room. He's talking to his father and I knew how important it was so I left them alone. Oh...' Brie turned her head. 'Here they come now...'

The concern in Anthony's eyes as he came into the room was almost like a physical touch for Elsie.

A hug?

'I thought you might need a bit of a break,' he said as Elsie stepped back to let both Jonno and Brie get closer to their son. 'A coffee down in the cafeteria, perhaps? My afternoon outpatient clinic doesn't start for a while yet.'

Felix's neurosurgeon came into the room at that moment, with a nurse carrying a kidney dish with drug ampoules and syringes in it. Elsie knew they would be in the way as things got busier so she touched Brie's shoulder.

'We won't be far away,' she said. 'Just send a text if you need us.'

Us...

Even walking away from her daughter, Elsie wasn't alone in dealing with this crisis, was she? It was a very new feeling, knowing that there were now other people who would be in Felix's life. Caring about him. Caring about *her*, even?

It felt as if their family was magically becoming bigger.

Stronger.

This new circle of caring went both ways too. Anthony was looking pale, Elsie thought. Shocked, even, and she had room in her heart to be concerned for how he might be feeling right now. He was seeing his son for the first time in many years. He had a grandson he'd only just discovered, but there was a possibility he could lose both of them in the blink of an eye.

He needed support as much as any of them so Elsie found a soft smile for Anthony as she followed him out of the unit. She even touched his arm to give them a physical connection for a moment—because the emotional connection they had right now was verging on being overwhelming.

'Do you think they'll have any sausage rolls in our cafeteria?' she asked.

St Nick's cafeteria did have sausage rolls, along with little mince pies and tiny quiches in the glass-fronted cabinets for hot food.

'No squeezy plastic tomatoes for the sauce.'
Anthony handed Elsie a small plastic sachet.
'I don't think Felix would approve.'

He'd put cups of coffee on the tray as well
as a hot snack for himself but it turned out
that they weren't remotely hungry after all.
Elsie found herself blinking back tears as she
remembered going to the café with Anthony
and Felix and how special it had been until
her world had quite literally started crashing
into chaos around her.

'I thought everything was coming right
too,' she told Anthony. 'Last night, Brie and
I were talking properly for the first time in
so long. She told me that Jonno had gone to
that music and movement class with Felix
and then they went and had hamburgers together afterwards and she said there was a
rumour that he might be applying for a permanent job in Bristol and...' she had to swallow hard '... I started thinking that it was the
right time to tell him that he has a daddy. And
a grandpa...'

'It will be,' Anthony said quietly. 'Soon.'

'But he's so sick... I had no idea. He was
a bit off-colour yesterday and we thought
he was coming down with something. Brie
thought she should stay home with him when

he didn't seem any better this morning but I still thought it was just a cold, which was why I agreed to fill a gap in the roster here instead of staying home with them both.' She dragged in a shaky breath. 'I'm so worried about him…'

'I know. But Jonno tells me his team are confident they're going to get on top of this. They'll take the shunt out and treat the infection with antibiotics. When he's recovered enough, they're looking at a procedure which could mean he won't need another shunt. He's in exactly the right place to get the treatment he needs, Elsie. He's got both his parents with him.' Anthony seemed to be blinking as if he needed to clear moisture from his eyes. 'And both his grandparents. I'm his grandfather…' he added slowly, his tone almost surprised.

'Of course you are,' Elsie said.

'No… I really *am* his grandfather, I think. Jonno told me that he never actually did a DNA test—he just said he did because he was so angry with me back then. Brie was there in the relatives' room at the time and she said she'd always thought Felix looked like Jonno and now she can see the Morgan genes even better. She said we were like peas in a pod with us all having the same eyes.'

'You do,' Elsie said softly. 'And they're lovely eyes. Such a warm, dark brown.' She looked away quickly then, suddenly realising she'd been holding Anthony's gaze far longer than was polite. And what on earth had prompted her to say something as personal as that?

Anthony didn't seem as if he'd noticed, but maybe that was why he glanced at his watch and made an excuse to leave. 'I should probably go and get on with my clinic,' he said. 'If you'll be okay?'

Elsie nodded. 'I need to ring my neighbour so she can let Dennis out for a bit. And then I should stay close to Brie. I know she's got Jonno's support but we've been here before, waiting for Felix to get out of Theatre and... it's not easy.'

'I know.' This time it was Anthony who made a physical connection by touching Elsie's arm. 'I'll pop in later, when I can.'

Anthony could see how exhausted Elsie was when he made a final visit late that evening.

'You really should go home and get a decent sleep,' he told her. 'Felix is stable now. His temperature's coming down. He's probably going to wake up tomorrow morning and surprise us all with how well he's doing.'

'I'm okay. When Brie gets back from having some dinner I'll go and have a lie down on the couch in the relatives' room.'

But Brie didn't think much of that idea when she came back into the room with Jonno.

'Go home, Mum,' she said. 'I'll call you if anything changes, I promise.'

Jonno could obviously also see how tired Elsie was. 'Are you okay to drive?' he asked. 'I could call you a taxi.'

'There's no need for that,' Anthony said. 'I'm heading home myself and I can drop you off, Elsie.'

The neat little end-of-terrace house with its pretty garden looked like just the kind of family home he would have wished for his grandson to be living in. And how lucky was Felix to not only have a devoted mother but a grandmother who was such an important part of his life.

'Thank you so much.' Elsie undid her seat belt as she spoke but her movement wasn't enough distraction to hide the wobble in her voice and there was enough light from the streetlamp down the road for Anthony to see that her cheeks were wet. Was that why she'd been so quiet on the drive home? Had she been crying the whole way?

When she shook her head it seemed like a response to his unspoken question.

'It's just the thought of going inside to an empty house,' she said. 'But I'll be fine. Dennis is there and…sometimes a dog can be the company you need most of all.'

'Would you like me to come in with you?' Anthony unclipped his own seat belt.

Elsie seemed to have gone very still as she met his gaze. 'That's very sweet of you, but honestly, I'll be fine.'

Anthony held her gaze, trying to gauge whether or not he should insist on making sure she really was going to be fine. He'd hate the thought of her going inside to cry alone with only the company of a small dog who couldn't possibly understand. Seeing the glimmer of those tears on her face was reminding him of when he'd found her in the park. When she'd touched a part of his heart he'd almost forgotten existed. Before he'd even learned of the connection they had. And now, thanks to Elsie, his son was talking to him again and he could see a future in which he wasn't entirely alone and that was making that part of his heart expand so much it almost felt as if it could break.

Perhaps that was why he felt compelled to reach out and use the pad of his thumb to brush some of those tears away from Elsie's eyes. To smile at her to try and convey how much she'd changed his life—in a good way—in such a short period of time.

She still hadn't broken their eye contact. She did move, just a little, by leaning her face into his hand so that he found himself cupping her cheek. He brushed away another streak of moisture, following the silvery track down to the corner of her mouth.

Maybe it was the way her lips parted slightly at his touch. Or the way her gaze was still holding his own. Perhaps it was just because it was the end of an astonishingly emotional, exhausting day and being even closer to another human being was irresistible.

Whatever the reason, the pull seemed to be mutual as Anthony leaned towards Elsie. And she leaned towards him? His fingers were still touching her face, cradling her chin as he got even closer.

Close enough to brush her lips with his own.

To close his eyes for a brief but oh, so delicious moment as he let time stop and the brush of contact became a real kiss.

CHAPTER FIVE

THERE WERE SOME lines in life that were an invisible boundary that couldn't be *un*crossed once you stepped over them.

You could pretend that nothing significant had happened—the way both Elsie and Anthony did in the wake of that late-night kiss in the car. It hadn't been long enough or passionate enough to qualify as being significant, had it? It had simply been a moment of comfort in the wake of a very intensely emotional day for both of them. Elsie had even managed to summon an embarrassed laugh as she offered a reason for that unexpected line-crossing.

'I think I need to stop crying all over you...'

'We're family now. Kind of...friends, at least?'

And there it was. A new line that felt safe.

'Definitely friends. And yes...if we share

a grandchild, that does make us family, doesn't it?'

'It does indeed. So you can cry on my shoulder any time, Elsie.'

'Nope. Not going to happen again.'

'Okay...'

The echo of that awkward conversation was at the back of Elsie's mind as she opened a cupboard to find her best—and largest—oven dish to put together one of her most familiar recipes because this was more than the usual family-sized lasagne. There were visitors coming to her house tonight.

New friends. Except, despite what Anthony had said that night, it was a lot more than friendship, really. Complicated bonds were being renewed, or formed, on all sorts of levels and Elsie was thinking about them as she layered her savoury meat sauce with sheets of pasta, grated cheese and béchamel sauce.

The line that the kiss between Elsie and Anthony had crossed wasn't the only one in the roller coaster that had started for both the Hendersons and the Morgans when Felix got sick enough to be rushed into hospital. Felix was blissfully unaware of some of the significant changes happening around him as Jonno began reconnecting with a father he hadn't ever been able to get really close to, at the same time as recognising how deeply in love he was with Brie. As far as six-year-old Felix was concerned, he'd wished upon a star and got the daddy he already loved and that was enough to make him the happiest small boy in the world. He not only had a daddy, he now had a grandpa as well.

He bounced his way back to being well enough to have a procedure that meant he didn't need to have another shunt inserted to drain excess cerebral spinal fluid and he was back home within a couple of weeks as everybody tried to get used to the new normal of those adjusted lines.

Jonno had started his new job with a helicopter rescue service by the time Felix had recovered enough to go back to school and he and Brie began coordinating their rosters so that they could spend as much time as possible with their son, to cover child care, medical appointments and therapy sessions or to be together to enjoy this special time of bonding as a new family.

Anthony had already decided it was time for him to downsize and, as he and Jonno got a little more comfortable with each other, an offer he'd made to let Jonno, Brie and Felix

take over ownership of the old family home
in a lovely, leafy suburb of Bristol was recon-
sidered and finally accepted.

To outward appearances, Elsie seemed to
be the least affected. She wasn't changing
her job or adjusting to new, important relationships like gaining a parent or a commit-
ted partner and she didn't need to deal with
the disturbance of moving to a new home. If
anything, life was being made easier for her
because Jonno's involvement meant less re-
sponsibilities in Felix's life. She was being
given more freedom to do whatever she
wanted to do with her own life. She could
work more hours at St Nick's or take on some
volunteer work with children or, perhaps for
the first time in her life, focus on herself and
not working nearly so hard.

With a final grating of Parmesan cheese
and some slices of tomato for decoration,
Elsie slid the heavy dish into the oven to bake.
She had a green salad to toss now and some
garlic bread to make but she found herself
pausing for a moment with a long baguette
in one hand and a bread knife in the other.

It was a bit daunting to know that she
would be living alone in a matter of only
weeks. Even Dennis was leaving. Not only

because both the little dog and Felix would pine without each other but he would be living with a wonderful big garden to play in and close to the forest park with endless exciting walks. Elsie needed to swallow the lump in her throat and get on with slicing the bread and spreading garlic butter. She wasn't losing the people she loved the most, was she? She was gaining more family, with a son-in-law she was coming to be very fond of and a...a co-grandparent. A friend who was also a colleague.

A doctor that Elsie had enormous respect for. A person she liked very much. The man who'd kissed her...

Not that there had been the slightest hint that Anthony had even given that friendly kiss another thought but, despite the visible drama of life changing so much for the people around her, Elsie was very aware that, while it might be completely invisible to others, something fundamental had changed for her as well.

They might have both been relieved to dismiss that kiss as simply a moment of comfort between friends but Elsie knew, for her, it was more than that. Because she couldn't forget about it. Sometimes, she even found herself touching her lips against her forefinger—a gentle touch that was no more than a brush but the ability that it had to retrieve the memory of Anthony's kiss didn't seem to fade. Worse, Elsie could also remember the way she'd felt just before he'd kissed her. When he'd been brushing those tears from her face and looking at her like that...

When she'd realised how much she'd *wanted* him to kiss her...

It had been years since Elsie had been kissed on her lips but it had been a very much longer time since it had had this kind of effect on her. Not since she'd been younger than Brie, in fact. Before tragedy and the busyness of life apparently stifled the ability to feel...

...attraction?

No. It felt like more than that. It was an awareness that wasn't going away. If anything, although Elsie was more than capable of keeping it completely hidden, it was getting stronger. Things were getting back to normal, with Felix back at school and Elsie back at work, but how she felt whenever she saw Anthony on the ward was anything *but* normal.

She noticed so many things about him now, like the colour of the shirt and tie he'd chosen to wear that day and the way he'd combed his hair to tame the waves. She could gauge the warmth of his smile so easily when he greeted her and that tiny beat of time that he held eye contact with her was definitely longer than you would with a colleague. Or even a friend?

She was also very aware that even thinking about that eye contact could make her aware of her heartbeat and that tingle of sensation that seemed ridiculous for a woman her age to be feeling.

Yeah…it was more than attraction. Elsie had to admit that she fancied Anthony Morgan. For the first time in…good grief, it felt like for ever—she had wanted to be kissed. She *still* wanted to be kissed.

Okay…a whole lot more than kissed.

How unfortunate was it that the man who'd sparked this level of desire was the one man she couldn't possibly consider going to bed with, even if he found her attractive. He was Jonno's father—a man who was now her daughter's chosen life partner, which made him pretty much her son-in-law.

Judging by the bottle of expensive French champagne Jonno was carrying when he arrived with Brie, bringing Felix back from his riding lesson that they all loved attending, the 'pretty much' part of that designation was about to change.

They all looked happy enough to burst.

And Brie had a sparkling new ring on *that* finger.

'We've got news,' Jonno confirmed, heading towards the fridge with the bottle. 'But we'd better put this on ice until Dad gets here.'

They were engaged.

To be married.

The son who'd told Anthony so many years ago that he wasn't going to follow in his father's footsteps and risk living the kind of lie his parents' marriage had been was grinning from ear to ear as he told the story of how Felix had helped him propose to Brie during his riding lesson that afternoon.

'We'd made a plan, Felix and me,' Jonno told them. 'Because we decided that if I'm his daddy and Brie's his mummy and we're all going to be living together in our new house very soon, then it would be a good idea if we got married before then.'

Anthony caught Elsie's gaze and he could see a reflection of his own surprise at how fast things were moving. Jonno and Brie were planning to move into the old Morgan homestead as soon as he moved out, which was only a matter of a few weeks away. Neither of them wanted to interrupt the storytelling by pointing that ticking clock out, however.

'So Felix had the ring hidden inside his boot,' Jonno continued. 'He told his mum that he might have a stone in his shoe which was making it hard to ride so she took it off while he was sitting on Bonnie and...'

'And she said, "How on earth did this get in here?"' Felix was trying to mimic the surprise in Brie's voice but it made him laugh.

'I realised what it was,' Brie said softly. 'And then I couldn't say anything at all.'

'I wasn't going to get down on one knee. Because...you know, what horses do all over the place.'

His wide eyes made Felix giggle again but then he straightened his face and his back as he shared his important role. 'But I told her that if my daddy and my mummy are taking me and Dennis to live in the big house then we were going to be a real family like my friend Georgia, and *her* mummy and daddy are *married*.'

'And I said I thought that was a very good idea if that was really what Jonno wanted,' Brie continued.

'And I said I've never wanted anything as much as this,' Jonno finished quietly. 'Except, perhaps, for Felix to get better when he was sick.'

He caught Anthony's gaze then, as if he was thinking of adding something else to that list. Like wanting to build on this new relationship he was finding with his own father? One that encompassed an adult understanding of how complicated things had been and a forgiveness that could allow them both to build something new. Better, even? Anthony had a lump in his throat that was making it a little difficult to swallow. He wanted that himself. Very much.

He had Elsie Henderson to thank for it even being possible to happen and her daughter to thank for making his son look happier than he'd ever seen him look. Ever...

Anthony had to clear his throat to try and get rid of that lump. He needed to distract himself from an emotional overload as well.

'I *am* better,' Felix said helpfully. 'And we're going to be a *real* family. You can come and live there too, can't you, Nana?'

Anthony took another sip of his champagne as Elsie responded carefully, getting up to check on whatever was in the oven and was filling the kitchen with a very delicious aroma.

'We've talked about this, darling, remember? I'll come and visit but you're going to be living in your special house with Mummy and Daddy and Dennis. I'm going to stay in my wee house here.'

'So Grandpa's coming to live here with you?'

Everybody laughed but Anthony could hear the embarrassment in Elsie's voice as she spoke hurriedly.

'No...your grandpa's found a lovely new apartment he's going to move into soon.'

Anthony was quite certain she was deliberately avoiding looking at him and that made him wonder if she wanted to avoid eye contact because she was thinking about what he was thinking about.

That kiss...

He still wasn't quite sure how it had happened. And he had no idea why it was so difficult to dismiss as nothing more significant than, say...a hug between friends.

No, that wasn't true, was it?

He knew perfectly well why he'd remembered it every time he'd seen Elsie since then.

And quite a few times when she wasn't anywhere near him.

He was attracted to her, that was why.

And it had only taken a brush of their lips to let him know that there was something very different about her. Something very desirable but also totally inappropriate, given that their children were about to marry each other. But they could be friends and he would make sure that she felt safe with him. It would be nice if they could both forget about that moment in the car that night as well. A distraction might help?

'It's not that much time to plan a wedding. Let me know if there's anything I can do to help.'

'It's not going to be a big wedding,' Brie said. 'It's just for us. We're going to find a celebrant and have a very simple ceremony— maybe at the beach or a nice garden. Felix will be there, of course, and we're really hoping you will both be able to come. We just need to look at rosters and find the first date that suits everybody.'

Anthony cleared his throat again. 'Are you going to get away for a honeymoon?'

'Not for a while.' Jonno shook his head. 'We think we'll get through the messy business of moving first and then we'll get settled into being a family and then we can all go on honeymoon together in a few months.'

'What a lovely idea.' Elsie was bustling about. She put a huge bowl of fresh green salad on the table and opened a long foil package and fragrant steam came from the hot garlic bread. Then she put on mitts and turned back to the oven. 'Maybe you just have a day or two to yourselves to celebrate your engagement, then. A night in Paris soon, perhaps? I'd be more than happy to look after Felix.'

Anthony saw the way Jonno and Brie looked at each other. He could actually feel the wave of love that flowed between them and how much they both loved that idea.

'We do both have this weekend off,' Jonno murmured.

'Let me sort tickets and a nice hotel for you,' Anthony offered. 'As an engagement gift. I'll help Elsie too. Between us, we'll be able to keep Felix—and Dennis—entertained for a weekend, I'm sure.'

'Can't I go somewhere too?' Felix begged. But nobody responded.

Elsie put a huge baking dish onto a trivet in the centre of the table. 'Dinner's ready,' she announced. 'Come and sit down, everybody. Felix, let's get your chair into your spot. Dennis, get out of the way—dogs are not allowed lasagne. Or garlic bread.'

'I hope I am,' Jonno said fervently. 'This smells *so* good.'

There was a happy, family sort of bustle as they settled themselves around the table in the Hendersons' kitchen and helped themselves to the food. There was still some champagne to finish as they continued celebrating the happy news of the engagement and imminent marriage and maybe that had something to do with the impetuous offer that Anthony found himself making to Elsie.

'Why don't you and Felix come and stay at my place on Saturday night?' he suggested. 'That way, Felix gets to go somewhere too. You haven't even seen the place yet and it would give Felix a chance to get familiar with it all before the move.'

'What…?' Elsie's fork had paused in mid-air. 'You mean staying at your house?'

He nodded. 'You could both choose your own bedrooms. My housekeeper would be delighted to get everything ready. It's a bit untidy with the packing I've already started but I'm sure we can work around that.'

'But…' Elsie looked taken aback. 'Brie and Jonno haven't even decided if they're going yet.'

Brie and Jonno shared a glance that made them both smile.

'Oh, I think we have,' Jonno murmured.

'We'd love to go,' Brie confirmed. 'Just a night or two would be amazing. We could fly out on Friday evening and be back by dinnertime on Sunday. If that's okay with you, Felix? Do you want to stay with Nana and Grandpa?'

Felix's eyes were wide. '*Yes*… At my new house?'

'We can visit.' Elsie's tone was cautious. 'On Saturday afternoon, perhaps? It would be lovely for me to see where you're going to live.' She smiled at Anthony. He smiled back.

'But I want to stay,' Felix insisted. 'So does Dennis.'

Elsie laughed. 'We'll see,' she conceded.

But Felix knew he was winning. He was beaming. 'We're going to have a *sleepover*,' he crowed. 'At my new house.'

Anthony and Elsie shared another glance. They were still both smiling but, again, he had the feeling that Elsie was thinking about exactly what *he* was suddenly thinking about yet again.

That kiss…

Nothing was going to happen, of course.

Because it couldn't be allowed to happen.

Not even in the unlikely event that Anthony was also feeling any of this level of…what *was* it, exactly?

Attraction? Anticipation? Desire?

An urge to jump someone's bones that was powerful enough to feel a little bit dangerous but, at the same time, more than a little bit pleasurable because Elsie had forgotten long ago how exciting it was to feel like this. But didn't that make it unbelievably inappropriate for a woman as mature as Elsie Henderson? Good grief, the way she found herself glancing towards the door to her patient's room, hoping to catch a glimpse of Anthony Morgan walking past, was the kind of way a teenager with a hopeless crush on the new boy at school might behave.

She needed to focus on the task at hand, which was washing the face of four-year-old Oscar when all he wanted to do was to go back to sleep.

'Being sick is quite a common side-effect

of the sedative they gave Oscar for his MRI,'
she reassured his anxious mother, who was
perched on the edge of an armchair beside
the bed. 'I expect he'll doze off again soon
and feel much better when he wakes up.' She
wrung out the facecloth she had dipped in
warm water and touched it to the small boy's
chin but Oscar pulled away and shook his
head.

'Would you like Mummy to wash your
face, darling?' she asked.

Oscar shook his head again. He pushed at
the bowl of water Elsie was holding, tipping
it over before she had time to step back.

'Oops…' Elsie put the bowl down and then
scooped Oscar away from the wet patch.
'Never mind, we needed to change these
sheets anyway. How 'bout you sit on Mummy's knee for a minute while I get everything sorted?'

Wrapped in a blanket and snuggled into
his mother's arms, Oscar instantly fell asleep
again. Elsie quickly stripped the bed and
headed for the door with her arms full of
damp, dirty linen to find that Anthony Morgan was not walking past this room, he was
coming into it.

There was no shirt colour to notice today

or a tie she hadn't seen before. Anthony must have come straight from Recovery or the ICU after a stint in Theatre because he was still wearing scrubs. He even had the disposable paper booties over his footwear and his hair was flattened from having been squashed by a close-fitting hat for a prolonged period.

And Elsie's heart did that skippy thing where it sped up and then dropped a beat to reset, because he looked far sexier in these baggy, pale green scrubs than he did in those beautifully tailored suits and shirts.

'Sorry,' she said, not quite sure what she was apologising for. The dirty sheets in her arms, probably, or was it in case he'd noticed her noticing *him*? 'I was just heading for the linen hamper.'

'Of course.' Anthony was smiling as he stepped back to let her pass. 'I've got the right room for Oscar Smythe, yes?'

'Yes…' Elsie hastily dumped the laundry and was back in the room by the time Anthony had introduced himself to Oscar's mother.

'I know there's a meeting tomorrow with the whole team,' she heard Anthony say, 'but rooms full of strangers can be a bit intimidating, so I wanted to come and meet you—and Oscar—before then.'

Elsie knew that smile would be reassuring the mother that Anthony understood just how scary it was to put your child's welfare, if not his life, in the hands of strangers but, if she was Oscar's mother, she would already instinctively know just how trustworthy he was.

'You're the heart surgeon the cardiologist told me about, aren't you? You're going to do the operation to take out the...' the frightened young mother closed her eyes and her voice dropped to a whisper '...the cancer?'

'The tumour,' Anthony corrected gently. 'We think it's unlikely to be malignant but we can't be completely sure until we can examine the tissue after the operation. It's most likely to be something called an inflammatory myofibroblastic tumour, which is very rare and usually benign. I'll print off some information about it and drop it in later for you and your husband to read. That way you can write down any questions you want to ask any of us.'

Elsie was busy smoothing a clean sheet over the bed and tucking it under the mattress but she caught the surprised glance from Oscar's mother. She smiled back, giving a silent response that yes, this doctor would actually find the time to do something like that. Because he was not only an excellent surgeon, he was a genuinely admirable person.

'They said something about the operation I didn't understand. About swapping valves?'

'The initial tests have shown that the tumour is growing in Oscar's heart. We know that it's not affecting the conduction system, which is good because it means his heart rhythm is normal, but we also know that it's affected the aortic valve, which is the one that lets the oxygenated blood back to the rest of the body. That's why Oscar's lips have been going a bit blue and he's been having the fainting episodes when he's exercising—he's not getting enough oxygen.'

Elsie pulled up the fluffy blanket with a blue teddy bear print and folded the top sheet over the edge. A couple of clean pillowcases and she would be finished in here, but she was slowing the task down because she wanted to hear what Anthony was saying. Not just because she liked the way he was making it easy for Oscar's mother to understand but in case it was all rather overwhelming and she might need Elsie to remind her of some of the things that had been said.

'We need to replace the aortic valve when we take out the tumour,' Anthony was saying now. 'And we've found the best way to do it is to swap it with the pulmonary valve, which normally takes blood from the heart to the lungs.'

'Why?'

'The heart has to pump blood pretty forcefully through the aortic valve to make sure it gets to the entire body, which means that a mechanical or donor or bio-prosthetic valve wouldn't last as long. The pulmonary valve is under much less pressure so it will last much longer—maybe twenty years or so and then it can be replaced again. It's called the Ross procedure. I've got some really good information on that too, with lots of pictures. I'm sure Elsie would be able to go over it with you later if she can find the time?'

Anthony turned to Elsie, an eyebrow raised, a smile tilting one corner of his mouth and…was it her wishful thinking or was he holding her gaze with what felt like almost a physical touch?

'Of course.' Elsie hastily broke the eye contact and fluffed the pillow on the bed with a little more vigour than strictly necessary. Again, she wanted to make sure that Anthony couldn't read what was going through her head.

That ridiculous teenage kind of thinking that it would be impossible to say no to anything this man asked of her.

Even if she knew it was something that could never be allowed to happen?

Something…intimate?

Yes, even that was a thought she could allow herself to play with. Perhaps *especially* that thought. Because she couldn't imagine Anthony Morgan doing anything inappropriate himself, let alone asking someone else to.

So it was perfectly safe.

And surprisingly delicious.

CHAPTER SIX

'So, DID OSCAR's surgery go ahead yesterday?'

'It did. Took most of the day, in fact, from seeing him pre-operatively to getting him out of Recovery and settled into the unit. His parents looked beyond exhausted by then, as I'm sure you would understand. But they were very relieved.'

Anthony was feeling quite relieved himself with the familiar comfort of slipping into work talk. It wasn't until Elsie had knocked on the door this afternoon that he'd realised he hadn't invited a woman, other than his housekeeper, into his home for…well… decades. It wasn't that he'd never had any female companionship over the years, he just hadn't welcomed them into his home. He had learned long ago how important it was to guard his private life.

This was different, of course. Because Elsie

wasn't alone and if anyone was going to be welcomed into Anthony's private life now it was his grandson. Felix's excitement over exploring what was about to become his own house and garden was making this visit a joy already but he had to admit there was more than a slight awkwardness between himself and Elsie. Especially now that Felix had disappeared from the lawn into the wooded area at the bottom of the garden and they were suddenly alone together.

Because Anthony had to be very careful not to step over any boundaries here. How horrified would Elsie be if she knew how attracted to her he was? To be honest, he'd been worried that his impulsive offer to help entertain Felix while Jonno and Brie were in Paris this weekend might have been a mistake, but Elsie was making this easy too, by letting him talk about something that put them both into a very safe space.

'It went very well,' he added. 'I love a complex case like that. The time it took to tease that tumour out of the interventricular septum and up into the left ventricular outflow tract and aortic valve only made it all the more satisfying. The icing on the cake, though, was the confirmation that the tumour was benign.'

'Oh…' Elsie's smile lit up her face. 'That's *such* good news.'

She was genuinely happy for her small patient and his family. The warmth of this woman was impossible not to respond to and Anthony was smiling back at her, basking in the glow.

Grinning, even…

'Grandpa… Grandpa…come and see what we found…' Felix appeared from behind the trunk of an enormous old oak tree, with Dennis at his heels, shouting with glee. He was walking fast enough to risk tripping over with his uneven gait but he wasn't about to slow down. 'It's a *boat*…'

'Do you know, I'd forgotten this was even here.' A minute or so later, Anthony was pulling ivy from the overturned rowing boat.

'Can I play in it?'

'It would need to be turned over and we can't do that until all these weeds are cleared away. I'm not sure that it would be much fun for Nana.'

'You might be surprised,' Elsie said. 'I love being outside in a garden.'

Felix was almost bouncing with excitement. 'Does it float?'

'I doubt it. It's been rotting out here for a

very long time.' Anthony helped Felix with the strand of ivy he was struggling to pull off the boat. 'There are probably holes in it under all this ivy and the pond is deep enough to be dangerous for small people. You remembered not to go too close by yourself, didn't you?'

Felix nodded. 'But I wanted to. Will you show me?'

There was a plea in that small face that squeezed Anthony's heart so hard it hurt.

'Let's have a look in the shed and see if we can find some gumboots that might fit you. Maybe some for Nana too?'

'Nana's got boots.'

'Yes, but they're her good boots. She doesn't want to get them wet and muddy if we stay out in the garden for a while.' Anthony led the way to an old potting shed, deliberately not turning to look at what Elsie was wearing on her feet. He didn't need to because he'd noticed everything about what she was wearing the moment he'd opened his door today.

They were the same long black boots she'd been wearing in the park that day when he'd stopped to talk to her. With jeans tucked into them again and this time a casual oversized knitted jumper in a shade of chocolate brown that was pretty much identical to the colour of her eyes. Anthony was wearing jeans himself and a very old black cable-knit jumper, which made it the most casual he'd been in Elsie's company but that awkwardness was still there. Even more so now, thanks to thinking about what Elsie was wearing. And about the colour of her eyes…

'Here we go.' The potting shed door creaked as he pulled it open. 'There's a whole pile of gumboots in here.'

'What's this?' Felix headed past the boots. 'Is it for fishing?'

'I don't think there are any fish in the pond. Lots of frogs, mind you. There might even be tadpoles at this time of year.'

'*Oh…*' Felix had gone very still, holding the small net on a stick in his hand and looking up at his grandfather as if he were a magician who'd just pulled something astonishing from a hat. 'I *love* frogs…'

'So do I,' Elsie said. 'My frog scrubs are my absolute favourites at work.'

She had a look of admiration in her eyes that was not that different from the way Felix was looking at him, but the real magic was that suddenly the awkwardness between himself and Elsie was gone. Not only that, there was a new bond between the three of them. Two grandparents and a small, happy boy. They were all grinning at each other—like a gang of small children planning to do something a little bit naughty but a whole lot of fun.

'There are some big old jars here. Let's put some boots on and go and see if we can catch some tadpoles, shall we? Maybe we can have a go at turning the boat over too.'

They all got muddy and damp and cold over the next couple of hours, but Anthony hadn't enjoyed himself this much in what felt like for ever. With a concerted effort they cleared the tangle of growth around the old rowing boat and turned it over to let Felix pretend to be a pirate until the lure of frog hunting took over. When they finally carried Felix back into the house because his legs were too tired, with Elsie carrying the jars containing tadpoles in various stages of turning into frogs, he found old towels to dry Dennis, lit the fire in a smaller room near the kitchen that had once been a library but he'd always used it as a living room and personal space to relax in, and then found more towels that he handed to Elsie.

'There's more than one bathroom upstairs

but I think Felix might like the big clawfoot bath in the bathroom near the bedroom he chose and it's going to be the quickest way to warm him up, I think. It might help those tired legs too.'

'I'm not cold,' Felix said, but his teeth were chattering. Then his eyes widened. 'Can the tadpoles come in the bath with me?'

'No…' Anthony laughed. 'They only like cold pond water. I'll look after them down here while Nana gives you a bath.' He caught Elsie's gaze. 'Have you got some dry clothes for Felix to change into?'

'I've got my jammies,' Felix told him. 'Nana said I didn't need to bring them but I put them in my bag when she wasn't looking because *you* said we could have a sleepover.'

Elsie's cheeks had gone very pink but, oddly, that awkwardness hadn't snuck back and Anthony knew something was changing between them. Something rather nice…

'I did say that,' he told Felix. 'But we'll let Nana decide later, shall we? After dinner? Are you getting hungry yet?'

Felix nodded.

'What's your favourite thing to eat? We could get pizzas delivered. Or fish and chips. Or…anything, really. Because this is the first time you've been here and that makes it extra special, doesn't it? Have a think about it while you have your bath and then you can let me know.'

It was Felix who had the pink cheeks when they came back down the stairs he insisted on managing by himself by sitting down and sliding, step by step. His pyjamas had dinosaurs printed on them and he had fluffy green slippers with claws on the toes, but even the distraction of the fish and chip dinner wasn't enough to dim his fascination with the tadpoles. He had one of the big jars right beside his plate with tadpoles swimming around in the murky water and Elsie had to remind him more than once not to speak with his mouth full.

'How long does it take for the bumps to grow into legs?' he wanted to know. 'And where does the tail go when it disappears?'

Anthony shared an amused glance with Elsie. 'Can you remember what that app was that was all about frogs? The one that little boy who'd had the bypass surgery for the aneurysm due to Kawasaki disease was so taken with? Didn't that have a really detailed timeline of the development stages?'

Elsie nodded. 'That's a brilliant idea,' she

said. Her smile suggested that she was remembering more than the patient. The conversation they'd had that day, perhaps? When
they'd both agreed how good it was to be single? When they'd connected as both parents
and grandparents, which had led to a very
special afternoon that Anthony wasn't ever
going to forget.

Felix fell asleep in front of the fire, with Anthony's laptop still open, inches away from
his face, still showing the animated trans-
formation of the tiniest tadpoles into fully
formed frogs.

'He's going to be dreaming about frogs
all night,' Elsie murmured. She found herself having to blink away a sudden mistiness.
'And it's going to be a memory of something
that he did with his grandpa that he'll have
for the rest of his life.' She was holding Anthony's gaze. 'Thank you for that,' she finished in a whisper.

He didn't respond immediately. Instead,
he picked up his wine glass from the coffee
table in front of them and took a long sip. Elsie's glass had barely been tasted. Because
she would need to be driving very soon.

'Do you know,' Anthony said slowly, 'I

once collected tadpoles for Jonno from that same pond and it was just as much fun as we had with Felix today. And then his mother came home. The nanny got fired shortly after that, presumably for having allowed Jonno to get so wet and muddy. The tadpoles disappeared the next day and she disappeared the day after that—with Jonno. I think they went to some child-friendly resort in Florida. Or maybe it was Spain. They were away for a month that time.' Anthony let his breath out in a long sigh. 'I think we both knew it wasn't worth ever looking for tadpoles again.'

Elsie could hear an echo of something Anthony had said to her about his wife that day they'd taken Felix to the park.

'*...if she thought he was getting too attached to me when we did get time together, she'd whisk him away on holiday. Somewhere tropical usually, with her latest lover in tow...*'

So he'd been punished for spending time with his son. For loving him.

'Do *you* know,' she said quietly, 'I bet Jonno still remembers catching tadpoles with you that day.'

For a long, long moment, Anthony held her gaze with a silent message of gratitude. And then he smiled.

'You're a very nice person, Elsie Henderson,' he said softly. 'I like you. A lot.'

Maybe it was the warmth in his tone. Or that his words were a verbal caress. More likely, it was that look in those dark eyes. A look that made her think that what had seemed so very unlikely was actually a definite possibility.

That Anthony Morgan fancied her as much as she fancied him?

Elsie could feel her cheeks getting very warm. Flustered, she pushed a stray curl back from her face to tuck behind her ear. She wanted to tell Anthony that she liked him as well. Definitely a lot. But she couldn't quite find the courage.

'I should get Felix home to bed,' she said instead.

'Or I could carry him upstairs and tuck him into bed here,' Anthony said. 'You could bring one of the jars of tadpoles and put it on the bedside table and then, if he wakes up in the night, he'll remember what we did today and where he is and he won't be frightened.'

'But…' Elsie's words died in her throat. Had she really been about to tell Anthony that she couldn't stay the night because she hadn't brought any pyjamas of her own?

But what if he gave her one of *those* looks again? The kind of look that suggested pyjamas might be the last thing she was going to need?

Oh, my…

Elsie picked up her own wine glass and took a gulp rather than a sip of a rather delicious Merlot. And then she took another because it seemed quite likely that she wasn't going to be driving anywhere too soon.

Or maybe she wanted to make sure she had a very good reason not to.

'…love you, Nana…'

'Love you too, sweetheart. Sweet dreams.'

Anthony watched Felix snuggle under the duvet of the bed his own son had slept in so long ago. He was smiling as he watched Elsie come to the door, with the soft glow of the night light behind her. He thought Felix was already sound asleep so it was a surprise to hear that little half-asleep voice again.

'…love you, Grandpa…'

His smile vanished. His own voice wobbled. 'Love you too, buddy.'

He didn't say a thing as they went back downstairs. He couldn't. What he could do, however, was to stoke up the fire and then find some more wine because by the time he'd refilled Elsie's glass the bottle was empty. When he had finally settled on the couch again he thought he could trust himself to speak without emotion overwhelming him.

'He's amazing, isn't he?' he asked softly. 'There's something about Felix that just creates joy for anyone who's lucky enough to be part of his life. I can't tell you how long it is since someone told me they loved me.'

Oh, help…maybe he'd been wrong about trusting his voice. He tried to wash the lump in his throat away with a mouthful of wine. He could feel Elsie watching him but he definitely wasn't ready to catch her gaze.

'Felix is lucky to have a grandpa in *his* life now,' she told him. 'And the more people we have around us who can tell us we're loved, the better.'

Anthony managed a nod. He felt safe enough to confess something, even.

'I know I wasn't a great father,' he said quietly. 'It was so much easier to keep a safe distance and focus on my work and providing for my family than getting caught up in feeling… I don't know…unloved, I guess. Not up to scratch or really wanted—as a proper husband or father, anyway.' For the first time since he'd started this conversation, he let his gaze catch Elsie's. 'This feels like a second chance. Perhaps I can be a much better grandfather than I was a father.'

There was something very like the kind of energy Felix was so capable of sharing in the way Elsie's eyes crinkled at the corners and the gentle curve of her smile.

'I'm so sorry,' she said softly. 'That you ever felt unloved. Or that you had to hide how you felt about your son. I can promise you'll get back any love you give Felix—in spades. And I can also tell you that you deserve it. I think you're one of the nicest people I've ever had the privilege of meeting.'

That did it. That warmth in her voice. That look in her eyes. And, most of all, the way she reached out to touch his arm, as if she wanted to underline the sincerity of her words with a physical touch. To his horror, Anthony felt a tear escape and slowly trickle down the side of his nose. He knew Elsie had seen it too, because she lifted her hand from his arm and caught that tear on her fingertip.

And suddenly they were back in that moment in his car, when he'd taken Elsie home that night and she was crying in the wake of what had been an exhausting, emotional day for both of them.

He'd known then that Elsie had already touched a part of his heart that was almost forgotten. A part that had been blown even further open only a matter of minutes ago when a small boy had said, '...*love you, Grandpa*...'

What was even more astonishing, however, was that he knew he didn't have to hide. Or be ashamed that someone had seen him shed a tear. That possibly for the first time in his adult life—at the grand old age of sixty-two—Anthony Morgan felt safe to let someone see who he really was. And how he really felt.

It was inevitable that they ended up in each other's arms, wasn't it? Just holding each other close. Sharing a moment that acknowledged they were both part of something life-changing. Potentially scary because personal relationships were not an area of life that Anthony had any great confidence in but...oh... this was a risk worth taking. He couldn't *not* take it, with that little boy asleep upstairs.

His grandson...

Maybe it was also inevitable that when they drew apart far enough to make eye contact it was another part of being in the car that night that was surfacing with all the subtlety of a runaway train coming towards something stuck on the railway track.

This kiss was very different, though. It didn't seem to be taking either of them by surprise. It felt as if it had been waiting to happen. Anthony knew, the moment his lips touched Elsie's, that he'd been very wrong in assuming she'd be horrified if she knew how attracted to her he was.

It *felt* as if she'd been thinking about this just as much as he had.

That she wanted it as much as he did. The tiny sound Elsie made as he deepened the kiss and his tongue invited hers to dance only confirmed what he was thinking. But as much as he wanted to pull her even closer and let his hand move just far enough to touch her breast, he had to stop. To pull away again.

For a long, long moment they simply stared at each other, and it seemed that an entire conversation could happen without a single word being spoken aloud.

We really shouldn't be doing this.

But any fear in Elsie's eyes looked as if it wasn't going to win over a level of desire that mirrored his own.

I'd forgotten how much it's possible to be attracted to someone.

Our kids would be appalled.

But the way Elsie caught her bottom lip between her teeth suggested that disapproval could potentially go the same way as any nervousness.

Is it any of their business?

I haven't taken my clothes off in front of anyone for so long. I'd be so embarrassed...

Anthony could almost feel her beginning to cringe. Preparing to run away?

Don't be... Please... You're gorgeous, just the way you are.

And then he spoke aloud.

'You're safe. I promise...'

CHAPTER SEVEN

MAYBE IT WAS true that you could only find the true magic in life by taking a risk.

By daring to step out of your comfort zone and taking a big risk.

By making yourself vulnerable.

And okay…that first time had had its moments of awkwardness. Acute embarrassment even, when Elsie knew there was no way to hide the changes in her body that inevitably happened as you got older, like the saggy bits and the wrinkly bits.

But in the end it didn't actually matter at all. It didn't matter that they were both more than a bit out of practice either, because any fumbling was excused by laughter and, when it really mattered, the need for this kind of intimacy and the astonishing reminder of the physical pleasure it could provide made any imperfections totally irrelevant.

It wasn't just the sex either, although that had been surprisingly good the first time and even better every time since. It had been decades since Elsie had shared her bed with anyone other than a wriggly grandson arriving for an early morning cuddle and she'd totally forgotten what it was like to fall asleep aware of another human's breathing and the warmth of their skin. How safe it could make you feel knowing that you weren't alone.

By tacit agreement, knowing how inappropriate this level of connection might seem to others—in particular, their own children—they had kept it a secret right from that first night.

Elsie had got up very early the next morning because she didn't want Felix discovering she hadn't slept in her own room and asking any awkward questions, or—worse—reporting the shenanigans that had gone on in his new house to his parents when they got back from Paris later that day. So she'd been in the kitchen, making breakfast when Anthony came downstairs. Felix was sitting at the table with his nose only an inch away from the glass jar as he watched his tadpoles swimming so he didn't notice the way his grandparents were looking at each other, trying to hide smiles that were both delighted but a little shy.

'How was your first night in your new house?' Anthony had asked Felix. 'Was it special?'

Felix nodded. 'I woke up but Dennis was on my bed and the tadpoles were there too, so I didn't need Mummy. Or Nana.'

'That's good,' Anthony murmured. His lips twitched and he seemed to be actively avoiding Elsie's glance as he cleared his throat. 'And you know what?'

'What, Grandpa?'

'I know I said that some things are extra special because it's the first time, but sometimes things get even better when you do them again.'

This time it was Elsie's turn to avoid catching his gaze but she was smiling as she turned to catch the toast popping up beside her.

Felix simply nodded. 'I like my new room,' he said. 'So does Dennis. And the tadpoles.'

The tadpoles were growing legs and their tails were shrinking fast and Elsie had to not only agree with Anthony that some things got a whole lot better on repetition but she was also realising that she wasn't too old to enjoy being a bit of a rebel.

There was an element of guilt, of course, in keeping a secret because she knew that what she was doing might not be acceptable, but Anthony had been right all along, hadn't he? What they chose to do in private, as independent single adults, was their own business. They'd both agreed right from the start that if or when either of them wanted it to stop, or things just faded by themselves, they would navigate that space harmoniously and not let any change in their relationship interfere with their involvement in the lives of their children and grandchild. They were clearly old enough and wise enough to be thankful for some unexpected joy in their lives but to also be able to let it go without the kind of angst it might have caused a decade or two ago.

And it was remarkably easy to keep it secret because it wasn't something that couldn't be controlled and, while it was impossible not to think about it a lot of the time, physically indulging in this astonishing new pleasure and satisfaction certainly didn't need to happen every day and it was no big deal when other things got in the way. And there were quite a few things lining up to do just that with so much going on in everybody's lives after Jonno and Brie returned from their romantic mini break. Moving house was always a big deal and nobody thought anything of the way Elsie stepped in to help Anthony not only search for but to move into the sleek modern apartment he found in the central city.

Both Brie and Jonno were clearly delighted that their parents seemed to like each other and they were grateful for the time they spent with Felix to help out with their own house move that had to happen around their work commitments. On top of all the disruption of moving, there was a wedding to plan and that took any focus away from just how much Anthony and Elsie might actually like each other.

Brie certainly hadn't noticed anything unusual. If anything, she was worried that her mother might be feeling lonely after she and Felix and Dennis had moved out.

'Are you sure you're not too lonely being on your own?' she asked a couple of weeks after she and Felix had moved out and she was back to collect a few final items. 'It must seem awfully quiet.'

'Mmm...' Elsie's response was accompanied by a smile. 'But I'm fine really... I know you're not far away and it's not as lonely as I might have expected.'

Not when Anthony had turned up on her doorstep last night, with a bag full of delicious take-out Thai food. When they'd spent the evening using the internet to share clips of bands from their youth playing favourite songs and discovered they'd actually been to more than one concert for the same band, quite possibly at the same time.

It was fortunate that Elsie was busy packing a shelf of Felix's favourite books into a box so that Brie couldn't read anything in her face. Like the memory of just how thoroughly Anthony had ended up kissing her last night. How they'd run upstairs to Elsie's bedroom like a pair of teenagers who couldn't wait to rip each other's clothes off.

How the touch of his hands and lips—and tongue, even—on her skin was becoming increasingly familiar but not even a little bit less thrilling. Quite the opposite, in fact.

Brie scooped up some forgotten plastic dinosaurs that were lurking in a corner of the room.

'That's enough for today,' she announced. 'We've got a couple of hours before Felix needs picking up from school and I need your opinion on something.'

'Oh? What's that?'

But Brie hesitated for a beat before responding. She was staring at her mother. 'Are you okay? Your cheeks are very pink.'

Elsie made a dismissive gesture with her hand, hoping it would make any memories of those hours with Anthony last night evaporate before her cheeks got any pinker.

'We've been working hard. But we're almost done.' Elsie pushed her wayward curls back from her face. 'You'll want to leave a few things here for when Felix comes for a sleepover so it still feels like his room. Why don't we put those dinosaurs on the window-sill?' She reached out to take them from Brie. 'What did you want my opinion about?'

'You'll have to see it,' Brie said. 'I've found a dress that I think might be the one for the wedding but I want to see what you think because it's not exactly traditional.'

Elsie laughed. 'Your relationship hasn't been exactly traditional either, so I suspect your dress is perfect.'

* * *

Brie didn't take her mother to anything like a bridal boutique.

'I didn't want anything frilly or white,' she said. 'I want something I can wear again and again that will remind us both of the day we chose to let the whole world know how much we love each other.'

One of the biggest department stores in Bristol had a section specifically for cocktail dresses and it was a real pleasure to be amongst the beautiful array of gorgeous designs and fabrics like silks and velvets and shimmering sequins draped on mannequins and hanging on racks.

Brie had the same mid-brown eyes as her mother but the streaks of lighter colour in her curly auburn-brown hair were gold rather than silver. She suited any earthy tones but her favourite colour had always been green and the dress she had found was a forest-green that couldn't have been more perfect. It was a simple A-line design but with a chiffon layer to the ballerina-length skirt and exquisite beadwork on the bodice that made it very special.

'Let me buy it for you.' Elsie smiled. 'As my gift.'

Brie hugged her mother tightly. 'Only if you let me buy *you* a dress to wear to the wedding.'

'I don't need a new dress,' Elsie protested. 'It's not as if I need to impress anybody, is it?'

Oh, really...?

That little voice at the back of Elsie's mind took her by surprise.

Wouldn't you like to impress Anthony? He might say you're gorgeous just the way you are but he's never seen you really dressed up, has he? What if he saw you and looked at you as if he really did think you were something really, really special? And even if there wasn't anybody you wanted to impress, how good would it feel just to do that for yourself...?

Elsie did her best to silence that voice by speaking aloud. 'Why don't we find a cute bowtie for Felix to wear? Maybe a bright red one to match the frames of his glasses?'

'Next time,' Brie said firmly. 'This is about you enjoying my wedding as much as I intend to. It's the only one I'm going to have, after all. Like you...' She threw a soft smile over her shoulder before she turned to start flicking through another rack of dresses. 'I never really understood why you never got married again, but I do now. I could never feel the same way about anyone else as I do about Jonno. You must have loved my dad *so* much.'

'Mmm…'

Elsie turned to another rack but she wasn't really looking at the dresses at all. She was trying to untangle a knot of emotion that was suddenly confusing enough to make her feel…guilty?

Not because she was keeping a rather big secret from her daughter, but because it felt as though she'd turned her back on Brie's father. For a moment, it was actually difficult to pull up a clear picture of his face in her head, let alone how it had felt to be with him. Were her memories being overwritten by what was happening with Anthony?

But, if they were, was that so terrible? It was more than thirty years since she'd lost the man she'd loved so deeply and right now it felt as if she were seeing the cover of a familiar book on someone else's shelf. She knew she'd loved it so much she'd never gone looking to replace it, but the storyline wasn't that clear any longer so she was tempted to read it again, just to remind herself of how it had made her feel to have her heart captured like that.

No…

Those confusing emotional strands were being smoothed out in her head, and her heart, enough to reveal a truth Elsie hadn't seen coming.

She didn't need to revive old memories to feel the intensity of what it had been like to fall head over heels in love because Anthony was capturing her heart more and more. Maybe it had started happening that very first time she'd spoken to him, when she'd sensed how deeply hurt he'd been by the breakdown of his relationship with his son. It had, without doubt, grown immeasurably stronger with the genuine care he had shown her when Felix had been so sick, but what had drawn her inexorably into the pages of a completely new love story had been their lovemaking.

Or was it a combination of everything? Of getting to know—and trust—a man who made her feel so cared for?

So…safe…

But *was* she safe? She knew that Anthony had no interest in a permanent or significant relationship. What would happen if she ended up having her heart broken? Would she have the strength and courage to do what she'd promised she would do and make sure it didn't have a ripple effect on the other members of their newly blended family?

'Look at this, Mum…' Brie's voice cut through, and fortunately short-circuited, that sudden fear. 'This would be the perfect colour for you.'

Elsie actually laughed. 'You want people to think *I'm* the bride?'

Brie shrugged. 'Who cares what anyone else thinks? And it's not white, it's pale grey.'

'Silver.'

'Okay…' Brie grinned. 'Pale grey that's a little bit sparkly. But it's amazing. Like something from the nineteen-twenties with that dropped waistline, but so elegant. And I love the long jacket that goes with it. Try it on, Mum. Please…?'

Elsie bit her lip. It *was* a beautiful dress and out of all the thoughts that had just been rushing through her head, one in particular had resurfaced—that desire to look her absolute best.

To impress the man she had fallen in love with…?

Or just to celebrate the woman she had become? Someone she could—and probably *should*—feel very proud of?

Whatever. The colour would be the perfect

foil for Brie's dress, it had been a very long time since she'd had a new outfit and it would be for a very special day.

Smiling, she reached out her hand to take the hanger from Brie.

Wow...

Anthony Morgan knew his attention should be firmly on the bride in her beautiful green dress and his son, standing beside her, in his dark, elegantly cut suit. It would have been quite understandable that he couldn't stop looking at his adorable grandson in his dark trousers that matched his father's, a white shirt and the bowtie—the same shade of bright red as the frames of his glasses, that his father was also wearing today, but no...

Anthony couldn't take his eyes off the mother of the bride.

Elsie simply sparkled, and it wasn't just the effect of that silver dress in the sunshine on a day that was perfect for a beach wedding. She was glowing with a level of happiness that was making her have to catch more than an occasional tear. And...was that his hand-kerchief she was using? The one he'd given her in the park that day?

He was tearing up himself, to be honest,

and not just because he could remember the way his heart had been caught by Elsie's grief over the loss of a small patient. Or that he was listening to the vows that Jonno and Brie were exchanging in front of the celebrant, with Felix sitting in his wheelchair between them and Dennis the dog lying beside the chair, a red bow tied onto his collar.

All those things were part of what made it necessary to blink hard to stop any tears falling, but they added up to a change in his life in a matter of only a few short months that was so huge it was a bit overwhelming.

He was part of a family. A *real* family that was not only making a formal commitment to each other on the beach today but he knew it was glued together with genuine love for each other—something he'd thought he would never have in his life. He had a relationship with Jonno that was getting closer than it had ever been before. He had the absolute joy of having Felix in his life too, but the totally unexpected icing on the cake was the connection he'd found with Elsie Henderson— the mother of his new daughter-in-law. The grandmother of his precious grandson.

A woman he was coming to care about on a level that went far beyond the enjoyment of her company or the deep physical attraction that was something else he'd never expected to find again.

Brie told Jonno that she had fallen in love with him even before she'd met him because she heard his voice so often over the radio and knew what a hero he was in his job. She told him that he had never known, but he'd been missed every day of her life since they *had* met, by both herself and then their son, because he knew that his father was a hero and he'd loved him even before he'd met him too.

'And when he did meet you, he started wishing on a star that you could be his daddy before he knew that you always had been. His wish has come true, and today my wish is coming true as well. I love you, Jonno. I always have and I always will…'

Yeah… Anthony was pretty sure that it *was* his hanky that Elsie was using to press under her eyes to catch those tears and he liked that. He would have liked to be holding that hanky himself, mind you. Or catching a tear with his thumb, the way he had in the car on the night he'd first kissed her. No…maybe what he really wanted was to be standing beside her and holding her hand, but that would have given their secret away and that might spell the end of the magic Elsie was letting him share.

It was Jonno's turn to say his vows.

'My life has been filled with adventures,' he began. 'But this…becoming a family and moving into our future together…this will be the best adventure I could have ever dreamed of. I love you too, Brie. I couldn't be happier that I'm becoming your husband today.'

'And Felix?' Jonno crouched down in front of the wheelchair. 'I've always been your daddy and I couldn't be happier about that either. I love you too. So much, it kind of makes my heart hurt—in a good way…'

Anthony's heart was hurting in a good way too. Full of love. For his son and his grandson. For his daughter-in-law and…

And for Elsie…

Yeah…this was more than enjoyment of her company, or the astonishing satisfaction that being intimate with her could bring.

He was in love with her.

He hadn't seen it coming. Perhaps because he'd never felt this way before in his life, he hadn't seen any warning signs. He might have ignored them anyway, because he knew that Elsie didn't want that kind of relationship. She'd already met, and then tragically lost, the love of her life and she'd never tried to replace the man who had been Brie's father.

It was one of the things that had made them feel so safe with each other because Anthony had never considered finding another wife. Why would he when he'd always have doubts that any relationship could ever be totally trusted? So he wasn't considering it now either—he just wished he could have felt like this about the woman he had married so long ago.

Or would it have only made things worse to be in love with someone who hadn't felt the same way? He could feel the edges of angst trying to muscle in on the happiness of this moment and he pushed back. How stupid would it be to let anything ruin this wonderful day? How right had he and Elsie been to agree how good it was to be past all the nonsense of romantic relationships and the heartache they could create.

'Congratulations,' the celebrant was saying. 'You are now husband and wife.' She smiled down at Felix. 'And still Mummy and Daddy. You are a family and I wish you all the greatest happiness that life can bring for you all.' She looked up, past the trio and the little dog right in front of her. 'For you too,

Nana and Grandpa. You're an important part of this family and their future.'

There were more photographs to be taken now, before the celebrant and photographer left them alone to enjoy the picnic they'd brought with them to this simple family wedding. Gorgeous shots were taken of a barefoot Jonno and Brie both holding Felix's hands as they lifted him over the gently breaking waves, with a happy small dog frolicking nearby. The young photographer suggested more dignified shots of the older generation, however, with Elsie and Anthony sitting on a large old driftwood log.

Close enough to touch, but that was okay because nobody could guess how much closer they had already become. Smiling at each other because that was perfectly acceptable in public, given that their family already knew they liked each other's company.

'You look stunning today,' he told Elsie quietly. 'I love that dress.'

He loved it even more now, because the soft folds of the coat she was wearing over the sparkly dress hid the fact that his hand was close enough for him to let his fingers tangle with hers as they smiled for the photographer. And for each other as they shared another glance.

'You know what?' Elsie whispered.

'What?'

'I'd rather be taking my shoes off and playing in the waves. Do you think that the photographer thinks we're too old to do something that fun?'

Anthony held her gaze for a heartbeat and he could feel himself falling into the softness of those brown eyes of hers. That warmth…

Oh, man…his heart was hurting again. Still in a good way, but there was a warning there that it could tip into something less good. If Elsie knew how he felt about her it would change everything, wouldn't it? She'd probably back off as fast as she could. Nicely, of course, but it would be different. And Anthony didn't want anything to be different. He wanted things to stay just as they were, for as long as possible.

But most especially for today. Today was a celebration. Of family.

Of love.

'I think we should show him that fun doesn't have an age limit.' His smile stretched into a grin. 'But we are definitely old enough to make our own choices.' He reached down to pull off his shoes and socks. 'I can't remember the last time I got sand between my toes. How sad is that?'

'There's no time to lose then.' Elsie had already slipped off her shoes. She dropped her coat beside them and caught the swirl of her dress into one hand. 'Let's go...'

CHAPTER EIGHT

IT WAS A rare occurrence for a cardiothoracic surgeon to be called into the emergency department of a paediatric hospital, especially when it was a trauma case being brought in by helicopter.

It was a first for St Nick's, on two counts. One was that it was a penetrating chest injury and the other was to have a father and son involved in the same case, at the same time. It was Jonathon Morgan who brought in the ten-year-old boy with a length of a metal reinforcing rod protruding from his upper chest and it was Anthony Morgan who had rushed down to join the trauma team, having been alerted to an incoming lung impalement injury with possible cardiac involvement.

It wouldn't have been surprising if the child had not survived the transfer to hospital but

Jonno was calmly giving the handover as Anthony arrived.

'Jack was playing with his friends after school on a construction site they'd broken into. He fell approximately two metres onto concrete blocks that had reinforcing rods poking out. Ambulance and fire service were on scene within fifteen minutes and pain relief and sedation were provided before the rod was cut. Air rescue was called in for rapid transport when both a pneumothorax and potential cardiac injury were suspected. He has a right-sided pneumothorax, current respiration rate of thirty-two and his oxygen saturation is ninety-eight percent on a rebreather. He's in normal sinus rhythm but he's tachycardic and getting frequent ectopic beats. I'm querying cardiac tamponade but didn't consider a pericardiocentesis. We've got bilateral IV access but restricted fluid resuscitation for permissive hypotension.'

Jonno caught his father's gaze for a moment, his hand still on the donut dressing around the base of the rod to help prevent any movement that could increase the level of injury. Anthony could see the concern that their patient's condition could deteriorate at any moment, along with the hope that the treatment they could provide here would be enough to save this boy's life. And maybe he also wanted reassurance that his emergency management had been the best it could have been?

Anthony nodded his approval. 'If there is a tamponade, it could be what's controlling any major bleeding from cardiac vessels.' He looked up from his first impression of the patient's condition and level of respiratory distress to the monitors above the bed, taking in the latest measurements of blood pressure and oxygen levels, the heart rhythm and respiration rate.

'Let's get a supine antero-posterior chest X-ray stat. If he remains stable I'd like a CT scan but we'll get a theatre on standby immediately. Jonno, are you okay to keep stabilising that rod?'

Jonno nodded. 'My shift's about to finish. I don't have to be anywhere else.'

Anthony stepped closer, to drape one of the heavy lead aprons over his son's shoulders so that he could stay where he was while the X-rays were taken. 'In that case, you're welcome to come into Theatre with us if you want to follow up on your patient. You could even scrub in and keep looking after that rod until it's safe to remove it, if you like.'

Through the doors of the resuscitation area they were in, Anthony could see an ambulance crew had arrived in the department and it was Brie who was talking to the triage nurse.

Jonno had seen them too.

'Brie was first on scene,' he told Anthony. 'She's brought in one of Jack's mates who also fell into the basement of the building, but he's been lucky enough to get away with only an ankle fracture. Could you let her know that I'll be late home? I'd really like to stay and go up to Theatre with you.'

Anthony passed on the message but when the images from the X-rays were coming up on screen as Brie went past, having handed over her patient, he called her back.

'Want to see?' Anthony invited. 'This is your patient as well. Jonno told me your crew were first on scene.'

Brie nodded. 'And it's not the first time I've been very relieved to have Jonno turn up,' she admitted. 'He'll be thrilled to be able to follow up with watching the surgery. Will it be the first time he's seen you working in

Theatre?' Her smile was a little shy. 'That's kind of special.'

It was time Anthony headed back into Resus to coordinate the next steps in managing his patient but for a split second her words distracted him because he felt surrounded by something he'd never had at work before.

The feeling of family?

He'd said something to Felix about the first time being special when he'd stayed with his grandfather—the same night that he and Elsie had made love for the first time. And now he was with his daughter-in-law—at work—and about to have his son watching him do his job for the first time ever.

Brie was peering closely at the screen. 'Oh, my goodness. That rod is right inside the heart, isn't it?'

'It's penetrated the right shoulder and lung and it looks like it's sitting in the right atrium. Could be through the septum as well and I'm concerned about the pulmonary artery. Hopefully we can get a CT and a better view of what's going on before we open him up. We'll have to put him on bypass. Your man might be rather late home.'

Her man.

His son.

Brie was the mother of his grandson and she had become his daughter through marriage and would be part of his life from now on. That squeeze on his heart, from the idea of family, was because it was growing. Changing to accommodate both the giving and the receiving of love.

'No problem.' She smiled up at Anthony. 'Mum's got Felix today and I'm due to finish before too long.' Brie turned away as her pager sounded. 'Good luck…'

Yeah… With the mention of Elsie and Felix, the last pieces of the family puzzle had just slotted in to create the full picture. Anthony allowed himself just another heartbeat of time to be aware of how precious that image—and everything it represented—was and how much it had changed his life.

And then it was gone. This case might be another thread that would bind his family together even more closely, but it was ten-year-old Jack who was going to have Anthony Morgan's totally undivided attention now, for as long as it took.

A few days later and the shared case became the topic of conversation amongst the group of adults sitting on the terrace of the old Morgan homestead. Felix was playing hide and seek with Dennis amongst the large shrubs in the garden. Jonno was getting the barbecue ready to cook steak for their dinner and Brie was placing a bowl of salad beside a basket of fresh bread. Elsie had just finished setting out cutlery and napkins and she sat down on the other side of the outdoor table from Anthony. She caught his glance for a moment and they had one of those rapid, silent conversations they were getting rather skilled at.

See? There was nothing suspicious in Jonno suggesting I picked you up on my way here this evening.

It does seem as if our secret is still safe.

Even if they guess they might not be that bothered, you know.

I wouldn't bet on it.

The best part is that I get to take you home again. You might want to invite me in...?

Oh, yeah... I think I might...

Elsie couldn't hide her smile so she made it about something else. 'Guess who I got as a patient on my ward today?'

'Who? Oh...' Brie's face lit up. 'Is it Jack? Is he out of intensive care already?'

'He's doing amazingly well.' Elsie confirmed the guess with a nod. 'He had a television crew in to interview him and his parents today. They showed me that picture of the metal rod spearing his chest that went viral on social media.'

'I had no idea his mates were taking photos.' Brie shook her head. 'I would have stopped them.'

'You were kind of busy keeping Jack alive.' Jonno smiled at his wife as she passed him a lager with a wedge of lime stuffed into the neck of the bottle, but then his gaze slid past her to rest on his father and the smile faded into an expression of respect. 'I wish you could have seen the way Dad handled that surgery. It was incredible.'

Anthony's shrug was modest but Elsie could see how much the praise meant to him. She loved that he and Jonno were getting closer with every passing week. The fact that she and Anthony were both here for dinner this evening so that they could hear all about the plans being finalised for the family 'honeymoon' holiday was a celebration of this new extended family that would probably make her tear up if she didn't distract herself.

'It's no wonder nobody can believe he survived the accident,' she said aloud. 'Or that everybody wants to know all the details.'

'I hope it will be used as a warning for kids not to break into construction areas and use them as playgrounds,' Anthony said. 'There's a reason they're fenced off.' He shook his head. 'He's one lucky boy, that's for sure. We went into that surgery not knowing what was going to happen. One wrong move could have been catastrophic.'

'Jonno told me all about it.' Brie was smiling. 'He's only just stopped talking about it.'

'Just getting him onto bypass and clearing the haemothorax was dicey,' Jonno said. 'But then the heart had to be opened and the rod removed. There was still the potential for a massive bleed at any moment. It was... tense...'

'I've never moved anything quite so slowly and carefully as pulling that rod out,' Anthony agreed. 'We had to repair the damage in the atrium and then, when we pulled it a bit further, that was when we found the pulmonary artery had been torn as well. If that rod had moved at all during transport we'd never have got him anywhere near Theatre.' He smiled at his son and then at Brie. 'You guys did an awesome job.'

'And now Mum's looking after him on the ward,' Brie said. 'How wild is that? I love that our whole family has been part of the same patient's story.' She stood up to walk to the edge of the flagged terrace. 'That's probably enough running around for now, Felix. Don't you think Dennis might need a rest?'

'We're being wolfs, Mumma,' Felix called back. 'We're good at running.'

'He'll tire himself out soon enough,' Elsie said. 'Or get sore. He's a wolf with a limp already.'

'Wolves…' Jonno was putting the meat on the barbecue '…are the new obsession in this household.'

'That's what we want to talk to you about.' Brie nodded. 'We've decided on the south of France for our holiday. As soon as Felix heard there was a wolf park we could visit to see them in the wild, he got super excited.'

'It's up in the mountains, near the Italian border,' Jonno added. 'But if we based ourselves near the coast, somewhere like Villefranche-sur-Mer, we'd have gorgeous beaches and all the medieval villages to explore nearby, with their restaurants and markets and all the history. I've already looked into renting a van or a big enough car, like an SUV that'll make it easy to take the wheelchair and everything with us.'

'We'll need a car,' Brie said. 'Because there's so much for kids in the area as long as we've got our own transport. Aside from the wolf park, there are some gorgeous parks and playgrounds, an aquarium in Antibes and the Gorges du Verdon, where you can hire kayaks. We thought we could rent a big villa—maybe with a pool—so that there's room for all of us.'

'Sounds gorgeous,' Elsie said. 'But it doesn't need to be that big, does it?'

'That's the other thing we'd like to talk to you about.' Brie shared a glance with Jonno before continuing. 'We want you both to come with us. It would make it a real family holiday.'

'A familymoon.' Jonno was grinning. 'Instead of a honeymoon. And we're not inviting you just so Brie and I can sneak out for a romantic dinner somewhere one evening.' He and Brie exchanged another private glance. 'Although that would be really nice.' His grin faded to make him look almost serious. 'We thought it would be great for us all, especially Felix. What do you guys think? Are you in?'

Elsie breath caught in her chest as she met Anthony's gaze. She could tell he was at risk of tearing up now. She was too. Because this couldn't be better, could it? A time where they could all be together. Having fun and adventures. Being close enough for long enough to really cement new bonds and lay solid foundations as they moved into their new future for their extended family.

'It sounds perfect,' she said with a wobble in her voice. 'I can't wait.'

'We'll get on with making the bookings after dinner, then,' Jonno said. 'These steaks are about done and I don't know about the rest of you but I'm starving...'

The familymoon was all they talked about over dinner, as they agreed on dates, how long they could be away for and who would look after Dennis. Felix was still talking about it when Elsie and Anthony went up to say goodnight to him after his bath.

'Did you know that wolfs have forty-two teeth? That's way more than grown-up humans have.'

'I did not know that,' Elsie said.

'And did you know, Grandpa, that wolfs live in families, just like people do?'

'I think I did know that.' But Anthony was distracted, looking up at the ceiling as Felix snuggled down under his duvet. 'Where did all those stars come from?' he asked. 'I don't remember them being here before.'

'Mumma stuck them up there,' Felix said.

'They were in his old bedroom at my house,' Elsie told him. 'There's a bit of a family tradition of making a wish before you go to sleep.'

Star light, star bright, first stars I see tonight,' Felix was happy to demonstrate. '*I wish I may, I wish I might, have the wish I wish tonight.'*

'I bet I know what your wish is tonight,' Elsie said as she kissed him. 'Does it have something to do with going to see the wolves in France?'

Surprisingly, Felix shook his head. 'It's about my baby sister,' he said.

Elsie's jaw dropped as she shared a startled glance with Anthony. Was there something they hadn't been told tonight?

'Mumma says it's not something I should wish for too much,' Felix added sadly. 'Even if my friend Georgia's mummy *is* going to have another baby soon and she's going to get a baby sister or brother.' He sighed heavily. 'Maybe I'll make another wish. About the wolfs.'

'That's a good idea.' Anthony ruffled Felix's dark curls gently. 'Sweet dreams, buddy.'

Perhaps the idea of Jonno and Brie adding to their family was giving Anthony and Elsie so much to think about as they went back downstairs that they couldn't find anything to say aloud. And maybe that was why it was so easy for them to hear the voices of their children, despite the rattle of dishes being loaded into the dishwasher when they were just outside the kitchen door.

'We'll have to find a place with at least four bedrooms. One for us, one for Felix and one each for my mum and your dad.'

'Do you think they're really okay with the idea of going on holiday together?'

'They seem to be getting on remarkably well. That photograph of them running into the waves at our wedding was quite something, wasn't it?'

By tacit consent, both Anthony and Elsie had stopped in their tracks. Wide-eyed, they stared at each other. Was Elsie wrong in thinking that their secret was still safe? It seemed as if Brie might be about to enlighten Jonno that there might be something going on between their parents, but the conversation appeared to have fizzled out as the clink of cutlery being dealt with suddenly turned into silence. Then, just as Elsie was about to start moving and lead the way into the kitchen, they heard a sound that could have been described as a groan from Jonno.

'They wouldn't,' he said slowly. 'Would they?'

'Surely not.' Had Jonno and Brie been sharing a long and horrified glance perhaps, as the very idea of their parents hooking up occurred to them? 'They're too old to be doing stuff like that. Old enough to know better, anyway.'

'I hope you're right.' Jonno sounded grim. 'Can you imagine trying to explain that to Felix?'

'I don't even want to *think* about it,' Brie said with a huff of laughter. 'It's so gross, it might put me off the idea of going on holiday at all.'

'And imagine how awkward it would be if something was going on and then it didn't end well?'

'I know, right? We might have to toss a coin to see which grandparent got to come to dinner. And birthdays and Christmas would be a bit of a nightmare, wouldn't they?'

Elsie didn't want to hear any more. She was instinctively backing away from the door. She didn't really want to make eye contact with Anthony but the pull was too strong. She needed one of those silent conversations that could happen in the blink of an eye.

Not that she expected any kind of reassurance, mind you.

It was going to be an acknowledgement that they were in trouble here.

A cry for help, even?

Dealing with an unexpected complication was something Anthony Morgan was well used to during surgeries and overhearing that damning conversation was kind of like a sudden bleed that could be fatal if it wasn't controlled very quickly, wasn't it? It needed to be clamped. Deciding how to fix it could come later, but doing *something* was urgent.

So Anthony caught Elsie's gaze to let her know he had this in hand. He cleared his throat loudly to advertise his arrival and then walked into the kitchen ahead of Elsie as if nothing was amiss. He even found a broad smile.

'I timed that perfectly, didn't I?' He ignored the guilty glance that flashed between

Jonno and Brie. 'Look at that, you've done the dishes already.'

Elsie came in a few seconds after him. 'Sorry... I meant to help with that.'

'It was far more important that Felix got a goodnight kiss from his nana and grandpa,' Brie said a little too brightly. 'Are you ready for a cup of tea? We can go online and see what we can find in the way of a villa to rent in France.'

'I should head home.' Anthony could hear the forced casual tone in Elsie's voice. 'I've got a day shift tomorrow so it's an early start.' Her gaze met Anthony's for no more than a split second. 'It's no trouble to get a taxi if you want to stay for a cup of tea and some internet surfing.'

'No... I'm not going to let you take a taxi.' Creating some distance suddenly seemed like a very good next step in dealing with this complication. Or was it that he needed to be alone with the only other person who was being directly affected by what they'd over-heard? 'I've got an early start myself and...' his smile was wry '...we're not getting any younger, are we?'

It was kind of mortifying that their children

apparently thought they were old enough to know better.

But it was almost understandable that they would be very surprised that people their age could possibly be having the best sex of their lives. Even more so that it would be horrific that they were having it with each other...

'Are you happy for us to book something, then?' Brie seemed to be giving the bench a very thorough wipe-down with a dishcloth. 'We were thinking of a villa that's big enough for us all to have our own space.'

Elsie was already turning away to collect her coat and bag so her voice was slightly muffled.

'Sounds perfect.' Her words were an echo of what she'd said earlier this evening but there was no emotion in her voice this time. 'I can't wait.'

So the unexpected bleed of the complication was clamped but Anthony found himself at a bit of a loss, as he drove Elsie back home, to decide on the best next step to try and fix things. If he was honest, he didn't want to think of how to start a conversation he didn't really want to have. Not when he knew the right thing to do would be to offer Elsie a way out. To give her the opportunity to not have to worry about how appalled her daughter would be if she found out her mother was sleeping with her father-in-law and the inevitable rift in his new family that would ensue.

The only way to guarantee safety, of course, was to make sure it wasn't happening any longer so they could stop keeping secrets and potentially telling lies. It had probably only taken that photograph at the beach wedding for the idea that something 'gross' might be going on to lodge itself somewhere in Brie's brain. Living in the same villa for a week, with the romantic backdrop of medieval French villages and gorgeous restaurants thrown in, it would be impossible to guard every glance or avoid being too close and, if that overheard conversation was anything to go by, the 'familymoon' would be totally ruined by the truth coming out.

He'd told Elsie it was nobody's business but their own but that wasn't true, was it? There were three other people involved, and one of them a small boy who wouldn't understand but could still be hurt by any fallout.

Anthony parked his car outside Elsie's house and killed the engine. He was thinking about the first time he'd done this and how, when he'd looked at Elsie, she was crying. He could remember exactly how he'd felt—as she'd found that space in his heart to nestle into. The space that had been far too protected to let anybody in for so long. And it had been a big part of the major changes that had made his life so much better.

It was all too obvious how much he was going to miss those secret, private times with Elsie.

Too much…?

If she'd been crying now, he wouldn't have hesitated to gather her into his arms and reassure her that they could find a way to make it work. But Elsie wasn't crying. And he knew better than anyone that you couldn't blindly trust that a relationship was going to work out long-term. He might have fallen in love with Elsie but he'd never told her that because he knew it would be an unwelcome pressure for someone who wasn't looking for a relationship.

For someone who'd found and then had to cope with losing the love of her life. She might even be relieved at being offered a way out, especially one where they could remain friends.

Where they could both be invited for birthday celebrations and Christmas dinner with their children and grandchild.

Grand*children*, if Felix's wish came true one day.

And there it was. A whole future that could be damaged and that would hurt Elsie as much as anyone else involved.

Anthony wasn't about to let that happen.

How hard was it to try and make this easy for both of them?

Elsie didn't know quite what to say. She needed to let Anthony know that she understood how important it was that he had reconnected with his son. That he had family around him for the first time in decades.

The first time in for ever, really.

He already knew how much importance she placed on his presence in his grandson's life because she'd been the one to tell him about Felix's existence. She'd offered him the chance to meet Felix and that had, in effect, brought the two of them together.

And, yeah…she was in love with Anthony, but she knew he might never trust someone enough to commit himself to a real relationship and, while their lovemaking had been unexpectedly wonderful, it wasn't enough to make it worth threatening these new and precious relationships he had in his life with Jonno and Felix. And Brie as his daughter-in-law, for that matter.

Elsie had had a taste of falling out with her own child in the wake of having secretly arranged for Anthony to meet Felix and she couldn't let that happen again. Brie needed her support as she settled into her new life with the man *she* loved and Elsie had been programmed to put her daughter's needs before her own for almost as long as she could remember. It had been a lifesaver to do so, in fact, when she was facing the trauma of having become a pregnant widow.

Anthony was such a gentleman, he was probably wondering how to redefine their relationship without causing any embarrassment or awkwardness. He certainly wouldn't want to lose his son again for the sake of the sexual benefits they'd added into a friendship. How relieved would he be if it was Elsie who made the suggestion that it would be better to go back to being simply friends?

What she really wanted to do was to invite him into her house—and her bed—for the rest of tonight.

She loved him enough to do the opposite.

'I don't want us to have to take turns having Christmas dinner with the people we love,' she said quietly.

'It was a bit of a wake-up call.' Anthony nodded slowly. 'We're lucky they were just guessing. That they don't really know the truth.'

'They *can't* know the truth.' Elsie's voice was a whisper. She didn't want to say it aloud, but Jonno had spent many years hating his father and the connection between them was new. Fragile. If it got broken again, it was quite likely it would never be repaired.

'I think the solution might be to create a truth that we don't need to hide,' Anthony said. 'That we're parents and grandparents and...friends. Just friends.'

Elsie swallowed hard. This was what Anthony wanted, wasn't it?

What he needed.

So she nodded.

'Just friends...' she echoed. 'We can do that.' She tried to smile but couldn't quite manage it. It was hard, but she caught his gaze. 'It has been...lovely, though, being... more than friends.'

'It has.'

Elsie could see the muscles in Anthony's neck moving, as if he was also finding it hard to swallow. She could see the way he was looking past her, to her house, as if he was thinking of suggesting one last night together?

Oh...how much harder would that be, knowing that every touch, every kiss, every shared glance with a silent message was never going to happen again? Elsie could feel the tears gathering and knew it was imperative that she got herself inside before she began to cry. Otherwise, it would only make this more difficult for Anthony and she wasn't going to let that happen.

She leaned towards him and gave him a swift kiss on his cheek. The kind a good friend could bestow without crossing any boundaries.

'Thank you for bringing me home,' she said. 'I'm going to go and see what interesting facts I can find out about wolves for the next time I see Felix.'

She didn't give Anthony time to respond, pushing her door open and scrambling out of the car.

If she moved fast enough—if she could get

inside so that Anthony would never know how hard this was for her—then, in the longer term, this would be so much easier for both of them.

CHAPTER NINE

I<small>T WAS AS</small> though nothing had ever happened, really.

Here she was, in the secure room for drug and medical supplies within the paediatric surgical ward, helping the most senior nurse on duty tidy up after an exceptionally busy day that had created an unacceptable level of chaos in an area that needed to be precisely organised. A perfectly normal task in a working day and she would go home for a perfectly normal evening. Alone.

There were no secret assignations to anticipate which would give her a thrill whenever she thought of them. Nobody to cook something special for or stimulating company to look forward to and oh, yeah…no sex that was better than any Elsie Henderson had ever had in her life—perhaps because she was finally old enough to know that it didn't actually matter if your body wasn't perfect and that it didn't have to be any kind of performance that you could potentially fail—it was simply a physical conversation to be cherished and, if you were lucky enough to find the right person—you might discover joy and a satisfaction that you hadn't even realised was possible.

But there was none of that in her life any longer and it was proving rather difficult to get used to its absence, which was a bit silly, really, after nearly a couple of weeks to adjust. Had she really thought that things like secret assignations and mind-blowing sex could be anything other than a fantasy for someone her age? Surely even falling in love should have been something she'd lost interest in long ago?

'Can you come and double-check the records with me, please, Elsie?' Laura was going through a set of keys in her hand, looking for the one to unlock the controlled drug cupboard. 'I want to make sure the numbers tally and get a requisition form off to the pharmacy to restock anything we're getting low on.'

'Of course.' Elsie picked up the clipboard where staff had to record details and sign for any drugs taken. 'Wow...we've had a few procedures needing sedation and analgesia today, haven't we? I helped with that central venous line and I heard about the spinal tap that was ordered. What else was there?'

'A naso-gastric tube insertion and a urinary catheter on two different but equally terrified toddlers.' Laura shook her head as she unlocked the door to the cupboard. 'Plus there was that severe asthma attack, and two seizures that weren't easy to control. That reminds me...' She glanced sideways at Elsie. 'How's your grandson doing? He was sick enough to be in intensive care not that long ago, wasn't he?'

Elsie nodded. 'He's absolutely fine now. He's getting very excited about a family holiday that's coming up. In the south of France.'

'Ooh, nice...' Laura was lifting cardboard boxes full of ampoules down from a shelf. 'I could do with one of those.'

'It's a honeymoon, really. My daughter, Brie, got married recently.'

'Mmm... I heard...' Laura's glance was curious this time. 'I'm not one to engage in gossip, but I couldn't help hearing something about your daughter marrying Anthony Morgan's son.'

Elsie's smile was wry. 'And they thought they were keeping it all so quiet. You can't beat a hospital grapevine for spreading the news, though, can you?' She bent her head, knowing that she needed to focus so that no mistakes were made in the important task of a drugs tally but she was also letting her breath out in a small sigh of relief. Thank goodness she and Anthony had been so discreet. If anyone had noticed that she and the esteemed paediatric surgeon seemed to be noticeably friendly, they probably just assumed that it was because their children had married each other. They were part of the same family now so it was…well…unthinkable that they would hook up with each other, wasn't it?

Gross, even…?

It hadn't felt gross at the time. It had felt more like something rather miraculous…

'It's a bit of a true love story, isn't it?' Laura asked a moment later. 'It's no wonder everyone's been talking about it. It's like one of those "true life" magazine articles.'

'Sorry, what?' Elsie's head jerked up, her heart sinking like a stone. She could only imagine how appalled Anthony was going to be if he found himself the subject of gossip in his workplace for a second time in his career. A fierce need to protect him followed the fear and the need to see him and talk to him felt like a physical pain.

'The romantic reunion.' Laura's outward breath was a satisfied sigh. 'Creating an instant family with the child that is actually their own.'

'Mmm…' Elsie let her own breath out in a sigh as well. This wasn't about *her*. Or Anthony. It was easy to find a genuine smile. 'It *is* a very happy ending. It was a gorgeous wedding too. Just a quiet one, on Sugar Loaf Beach.'

She turned a page on the clipboard, looking for the page for the controlled drugs like morphine and fentanyl and midazolam that had to be behind two separate locks, but she'd been distracted into thinking about something very different that she'd been sorting through just yesterday evening. Having found a very pretty silver heart-shaped frame when she'd been out shopping in the afternoon, she had wanted to choose a photograph of that special day on Sugar Loaf Beach to put into it.

Unexpectedly, it had turned out to be a far from easy choice. Did she want the stunning picture of Brie and Jonno looking into each other's eyes as they exchanged their vows, with Felix between them and gazing up at both of his parents adoringly? Or the one where they were swinging Felix above the foam of a breaking wave and clearly all laughing with the joy of both the setting and the occasion?

Maybe the one she really wanted to go on her bedside table was the one of herself sitting with Anthony on that driftwood log and they were smiling at each other. Elsie would never forget that his fingers were tangled with her own in that moment, hidden beneath the folds of that beautiful silver dress. Even now when he was nowhere near her, she could feel exactly how she'd felt with that touch—both physical from his hand and oh, so emotionally from losing herself in the way he was looking at her.

As if he was as much in love with her as she had been with him?

No...she couldn't think of that in the past tense. You couldn't feel like that about someone and have it just evaporate like magic because it wasn't convenient.

'Must be a bit weird for you, though. With Anthony?'

Elsie made a noncommittal sound that could have been amusement, but it actually was a bit weird now. Because it was when she saw him on the ward or passed him in a hospital corridor that it really felt as if nothing so deeply intimate had ever happened between them. As if they were merely colleagues. Friends. And…he looked perfectly happy. As though calling it quits on their secret relationship wasn't bothering him at all.

That he might, as she'd suspected, be relieved that they could dial things back to something that couldn't go wrong and threaten his new relationship with his son and grandson?

The columns that held the time of day, drug name, dosage and signature of the person removing it blurred in front of Elsie's eyes and, for a horrible moment, she thought she might burst into tears. This was a roller coaster she really, really wanted to get off.

But Laura was smiling. 'I mean, he's a wonderful doctor and his patients' families think he's marvellous, but Anthony Morgan's a bit…um…aloof, isn't he?'

Aloof…?

Elsie shook her head by way of a response this time.

'Not really,' was all she said. It was time they got stuck into the job at hand. 'I've got a total of six ampoules of morphine listed as used today. That means there should still be twelve in the box.'

The glass ampoules rattled as Laura counted them and Elsie waited for the tally with that word still echoing in the back of her head.

Aloof meant distant, didn't it? Unfriendly. Uncaring, even?

She was taken back to the very first time she'd spoken to him, in the early hours of that morning when she'd been so surprised to find him in the staffroom. Yes…she would never have described him as being particularly social. He did his job and he did it extremely well, but you could see his personal boundaries a mile off. She could remember the way he'd shut her out as soon as she'd asked a question about one of his patients that she might not have been entitled to ask. She could remember how emotional he'd seemed when he'd seen that photograph of Jonno in the newspaper. He was a private person, certainly, but then he'd had good reason to learn to be like that, hadn't he? She could even remember thinking that he was the kind of man who could keep a secret for ever if he needed to.

But aloof…?

In another lightning-fast thought process, Elsie could remember the way he'd looked at her in the car that night. The concern in his eyes because she was crying. The way he'd touched her so much more deeply than simply on her lips when he'd given her that gentle kiss. The way he'd kissed her that night in front of the fire and, later, the way he'd made it so easy—joyous, even—to rediscover a kind of intimacy she'd thought only happened to other people. Much younger people…

No. Anthony Morgan wasn't aloof. He was an intelligent, gentle, caring man who'd been so badly hurt in his private life that he was afraid to trust that it wasn't about to happen again and…

She loved him, for all those reasons and more.

…and she was missing him so much that it hurt.

The morphine ampoules tallied. So did the fentanyl, midazolam and ketamine. They quickly checked the antibiotics and steroids and a dozen other drugs and then they both signed the charts to record their findings. Then Laura looked at her watch.

'It's nearly time for shift change. I'll go and get the requisition form done for the pharmacy if you want to go and check your patients before handover. Someone on night shift can do a stocktake of the IV supplies and dressings.'

'Thanks. I don't want to be late home today. Brie's dropping Felix around because both she and Jonno are working night shifts. I've been looking forward to it all week.'

'You must be missing him terribly,' Laura sympathised.

'I am.' Elsie's response was heartfelt. And she wasn't just talking about her grandson.

'Nana… Nana…we're *here*…'

'I think Nana knows that, Felix.' It felt like too long since Brie had stepped through the front door of her childhood home. 'Dennis, be quiet! You won't be welcome here if you keep making a noise like that.'

But her mother didn't seem to be minding when Brie got to the kitchen to find Elsie crouched down getting one of Felix's fiercest hugs, with Dennis trying to push in to get his share of the love.

'It's a sleepover,' Felix was telling his grandmother.

'It is. Did you remember to bring your PJs? And your favourite stories?'

Felix nodded. 'Mumma said I couldn't take the stars off the ceiling, though.'

'That's okay. Remember we left one behind, right above your pillow, just for special nights like this, so you can still make a wish?'

She was smiling as she looked up to see Brie come into the kitchen, but her smile faded so fast Brie knew she wasn't doing the best job in hiding her thoughts. She found herself blinking fast too, in the hope of making sure no tears were forming.

Felix hadn't noticed anything amiss. He was grinning from ear to ear as he finally stopped trying to strangle his grandmother. 'There's a surprise, Nana.' He was clutching his favourite soft toy horse that was the star of the series of Nobby the pony books he loved so dearly. 'Nobby isn't a cowboy pony any more.'

'Isn't he?' Elsie managed to sound excited about stories they all knew by heart, having had to read them aloud to Felix on a nightly basis. 'Did he go back to the circus?'

'No.' It was Brie who answered. 'You're not going to believe this. Nobby's—'

'Don't tell her,' Felix ordered. 'I'm going

to hide it under my pillow so it's a proper surprise.'

Brie handed him his backpack so he could find the precious book and then he was gone. They could hear his slow but determined progress up the stairs a few seconds later, his backpack thumping on each step behind him.

'Got time for a cuppa?' Elsie asked. 'I just made a pot of tea.'

'I guess.' Brie couldn't sound as cheerful as she was trying to. She couldn't help the sigh that escaped as she sat down at the kitchen table either.

'What is it, love?'

'Nothing. I'm just a bit tired. It's not helping that I seem to have picked up a bit of that tummy bug Felix had last week.' Brie knew she wasn't fooling her mother, but she could at least try and distract her. 'There's a position on a new shift coming available. A daytime one which would fit much better with school hours and I wouldn't have to do any night shifts. I've applied for it, so keep your fingers crossed for me, Mum.'

'I will.' Elsie put a mug of tea in front of Brie. 'Do you want me to check on Felix and watch him coming down the stairs?'

She shook her head. 'We've got stairs too,

remember? He's got a new technique of sliding down on his bottom instead of coming down backwards, which he thinks is great fun.'

Elsie sat down and picked up her own mug but she was looking up at the ceiling. 'He's taking a long time putting that book under his pillow.'

'He's probably reading it for the millionth time. I shouldn't spoil the surprise, but Nobby's having a holiday at a riding school and there's a little disabled boy who's always been too scared to ride. I won't tell you the ending but Felix thinks the whole story is about him.'

'Aww...' Elsie's smile was misty. 'I can't wait.'

'I should warn you about the wish too. Just so you know what to say.'

'He's not still wishing for a little brother or sister, is he? Like Georgia's getting?'

Brie's jaw dropped. 'How did you know that?'

'He told me. And Anthony. That night we were both there for the barbecue?'

'You didn't say anything.'

'No...'

The odd look on her mother's face made Brie wonder if there was something going on that she'd missed. 'You and Anthony haven't even been around at the same time since then, come to think of it.'

'Haven't we?' Was it her imagination or was Elsie avoiding meeting her gaze? 'We'll make up for it with our time in France when we're all together. That's only a few weeks away now.'

'I know.' Brie nodded. And then, to her horror, she felt a tear escape.

'Oh, love…' Elsie reached to pull a few tissues from a box at the end of the table. 'I knew there was something more than just being tired. What is it?'

'I don't think it's just Felix who wants a little brother or sister. I'm pretty sure Jonno wants another baby too.'

'Oh…' This time, it was a sound of trepidation.

'I can't do it, Mum. I couldn't face going through another pregnancy.'

She could see that Elsie understood exactly why. Of course she did. She'd been through every moment with her, from the shock of learning of the accidental pregnancy to the terrifying experience of having her baby operated on before he was even born. Good grief, Elsie had even mortgaged her house to pay for the in utero surgery that they'd had to travel overseas to access.

'Jonno thinks he understands how difficult it was,' Brie added quietly. 'And I know he was there when Felix got the infection and had those awful seizures and needed the surgery but…'

'But he can't really know how terrifying it would be to take that risk again,' Elsie finished for her.

'He did say the risk of having a second child with a neural tube defect is very small— only about four percent.' Brie had to catch another tear. 'But that sounds like a huge risk to me. And what if it *can* be detected a lot earlier than it was for Felix? I wouldn't want to be faced with being offered a termination again. Do you remember how heartbreaking that was?'

Elsie was nodding. There were tears in *her* eyes too. 'I'm so sorry, love,' she said softly. 'This should be such a happy time for you all. I hate that you're having to think about this.'

'It *is* a happy time.' Brie blew her nose. She could hear the thump of Felix beginning to slide down the staircase. 'And Jonno hasn't actually said anything other than that he heard Felix making a wish that isn't even unreasonable.' She sniffed and blinked away the last of any tears. 'I got the feeling that Jonno thinks it would complete our family, and it *would*. And it's not that I don't want another baby. I just don't think I could do it, and that makes me feel like I'm letting him down...'

'You're not.' Elsie reached to put her hand over Brie's. 'He's got a whole new, amazing life thanks to you. You both adore each other. He's got the most amazing son he could ever wish for. He's got his own dad back in his life and he's living in the home he grew up in again. These are all huge changes. Wonderful changes. When he's had a bit of time to get used to them all, he'll realise it's more than enough. I'm sure he would never expect you to do something that would be so traumatic.'

'He wouldn't. But...oh, Mum...you should have seen the look in his eyes when he told me what Felix was wishing for... I just know how much he wants it too and I love him so much that a big part of me wants to give him exactly what he wants.'

'Are you talking about me?' Felix appeared at the kitchen door, with Dennis at his heels. 'What *do* I want?'

'A biscuit?' Elsie suggested brightly, hurriedly getting to her feet. 'I think there's just enough time before dinner for you to have one. I made chocolate chip biscuits last night.'

'A chippy bickie.' Felix licked his lips. 'Can Dennis have one too?'

'No.' Brie also got to her feet. 'Come and give me a kiss, darling. I've got to go to work. I'll be back in the morning in time to take you to school.'

A tetralogy of Fallot was a complex cardiac condition in that it involved four different but related defects that interfered with how much oxygenated blood could be pumped around the body.

Anthony Morgan had first met Jemma when she was only a couple of months old and her parents noticed how blue she was becoming when she cried for a prolonged period of time. Having been born slightly prematurely, she had been too small for a complete repair but a less invasive procedure had been done to improve her blood flow.

Now, more than a year later, Anthony had spent several hours in Theatre already, with confidence that his work today would let this little girl live a full life with a very good long-term outlook. He had patched the hole between the ventricles and removed the obstruction to the flow of blood to the lungs by enlarging both the pulmonary valve and the associated arteries. They were now ready for the crucial step in the surgery of taking Jemma off the cardiac bypass machine that had allowed the heart to be disconnected from the body's circulation while the delicate work to repair the defects had been done.

The rewarming of Jemma's body had begun, the aortic cross clamp was removed to allow the heart to re-join the circuit of blood flow and air was removed from the chambers of the heart. Using internal paddles with a small electrical charge to restart the heart and reinflating the lungs were part of a stepped algorithm that was automatic to follow, but difficulty in weaning a patient off bypass successfully was not that unusual and Anthony had to be prepared to deal with any complications.

It wasn't until he had closed the chest and Jemma was safely in Recovery with all monitored parameters within acceptable limits that Anthony could feel both his focus and that tension finally drop to a level that was low enough to allow anything else some space in his head. It was in that moment, as he turned to walk out through the swing doors of the recovery area, that the first thought of Elsie Henderson snuck into his mind.

Well, no…that wasn't entirely true. It was always one of the first thoughts he had every single day, when he woke up in that huge bed. Alone. It had become automatic to think of her again when he walked into the pristine kitchen area of his new apartment to make a coffee before heading to work, because he couldn't help comparing this sleek and impersonal modern design with the cosy warmth of the little kitchen in Elsie's old, terraced house. Anthony was increasingly hating his new home but, in a way, that was a good thing. It was close to the hospital and work had always been his escape from the disturbing emotional aspects of a life that was less than ideal in other areas.

He wasn't about to let himself get too hung up on where he lived either, because he had so much in his life to be very thankful for. He and Jonno were getting closer with every passing week and he was a firm part of his delightful grandson's life now. He dropped in at least once a week to spend time with Felix, often out in the garden where Jonno would sometimes help with what needed to be done.

Felix had another jarful of tadpoles on the go and Brie was always welcoming. His daughter-in-law had a soul as warm as her mother's, Anthony had decided, and she was genuinely happy that he and Jonno had not only reconnected, they were building a better relationship than they'd ever had in the past.

What was wrong with him, he wondered as he pressed the lift button that would take him down to the ward for a quick round of his inpatients? With so many amazing things in his life that he'd never dreamt of having, why wasn't he the happiest man on the planet? Why was it such a relief when he had a day that included complex surgery that precluded any kind of personal reflection for many hours on end?

Because it felt as if something was missing?

Because he was missing Elsie so very much?

It wasn't as if the feeling was mutual. He'd probably hit the nail on the head when he'd thought that Elsie needed to be offered a way out of the intimate relationship they'd somehow fallen into so unexpectedly in order to protect what was most important to her— her daughter and her grandson. She certainly looked happy enough every time he saw her at work these days and he couldn't help thinking that it might be a deliberate move on her part not to turn up to their children's home at the same time.

Finding her in Jack's room when he went in a few minutes later was bittersweet. Just being this close to her was filling a tiny part of that huge space her absence had left in his life, but it was like stepping back into his past. He needed to pull defensive walls around him and put on a performance that was capable of making how he felt undetectable.

'Look, Jack, it's Dr Morgan. I told you he'd be here as soon as he could.' Elsie's smile filled another part of that space in his heart. 'Jack's hanging out to get the final okay that he can go home today.'

'I know.' Anthony managed to return the smile with warmth that was equally genuine, but he cut the eye contact before it became even a heartbeat too long to be normal for a space between colleagues and friends. 'Sorry, Jack. I had a bit of a long operation to do. That's why I'm still wearing my scrubs.'

'How come your scrubs don't have frogs on

them, like Elsie's?' ten-year-old Jack wanted to know.

Anthony shrugged. 'Maybe I'm a bit too boring for frogs.'

'That's not true.' Elsie winked at Jack. 'I happen to know that Dr Morgan has *real* frogs in his garden. Sometimes, he even has tadpoles in a jar in his kitchen.'

Jack's jaw dropped. 'How do you know that?'

'We're kind of friends.' Anthony had seen a flash of something like panic in Elsie's eyes. Did she think she might have overstepped a boundary? Or that Jack's mother might say something to someone else on the ward that would start the rumour mill churning? He wanted to reassure her that it wasn't a problem but avoided looking in her direction as he spoke, however. Perhaps he didn't want to see any relief or the nod that might back up his bland description of any connection between them?

Jack's mother was more than ready to back him up. 'People that work together are often friends, Jack. And you could follow Dr Morgan's example. Doing something like going out looking for tadpoles with your mates would be a much better idea than breaking into building sites.'

Jack was scowling now. 'They'd think I was just a stupid kid. Or a scaredy cat.'

'I don't think so,' Elsie said. 'I bet they've all seen you on TV or the internet. You'll be a bit of legend. Maybe you can be someone whose example they can follow.'

'You could have died, Jack,' his mother said quietly. 'Dr Morgan saved your life. Friends that let that kind of thing happen aren't the kind of friends you need, if you ask me.'

Anthony tilted his head to catch Jack's gaze. 'You'll figure it out,' he told the boy. 'Right now I'd like to see how well your wound is healing. Could you unbutton your pyjama top for me?'

Jack complied. 'They took some stitches out today.'

'I know. That was the hole that was there for the chest drain. You don't need to get any stitches out from the main incision. They just melt away under the skin.' Anthony was looking at the wound on the centre of Jack's chest, gently pressing on the skin. 'This is healing nicely.' He looked up at Jack's mother. 'Keep an eye out for any redness or ooze or if Jack starts running even a bit of a temperature.

Anything over thirty-seven point five and you should go and see your family doctor or come into the emergency department here at St Nick's.'

'Thanks, Dr Morgan. They said he can go back to school in a week or two, is that right?'

'Yes, but you'll need to be careful with the weight of the schoolbag he's carrying and make sure it's not over two kilograms. Has the physiotherapist been in to give you some exercises to do at home?'

She nodded. 'She said it's really important to do them to stop any stiffness in his neck or shoulders. And the breathing exercises to keep his lungs clear.'

Elsie had the discharge papers ready to be signed. 'Have you seen the pre-discharge results from the chest X-ray and ECG and the echo that got done this morning?'

'I have.' Anthony's smile was for Elsie this time but he turned swiftly to Jack's mother. 'And they're all looking reassuringly normal. We've set up an appointment with the cardiology department for Jack in a month's time, just to keep an eye on him, but do remember you can come in any time you're worried, like if he seems unusually tired or short of breath or something.'

'So I can go home now?' Jack asked.

'You can. But you still need to be a bit careful. You've got wires holding the bone in the front of your chest together. The sternum.' He touched Jack's chest again. 'If you put your fingers here you can feel the little bumps where they're healing.'

It was no surprise that it felt irresistible to lift his gaze to catch Elsie's right then. Anthony was never going to forget the drama of that day they'd first worked together, opening Vicky's little chest to try and save her life. With merely a split second of eye contact, he knew that Elsie was thinking about that same tragic scenario and he knew that it was still enough to distress her.

He also knew in that same fraction of time that they hadn't lost the ability to have a lightning-fast telepathic conversation.

We did the best we possibly could.

I know.

I'll never forget it either.

I know...

Of course she did. And it was only one of the threads of connection that had bound them together so easily.

And so intimately.

It felt as if they both looked away at exactly the same time.

'It needs twelve weeks for the sternum to heal properly,' Anthony told Jack. 'You need to avoid any jarring movements like jumping, and any twisting like you might get if you play football or use a skateboard. Don't use just one arm to pull or push anything either.' He turned to Jack's mother. 'It might still be uncomfortable for a while but paracetamol should be enough to deal with it.' He took a pen from the pocket of his scrub tunic and scribbled his signature on the discharge form.

'Take care of yourself,' he said to Jack. 'I don't ever want to see you coming into my hospital with anything else poking out of your chest, okay?'

'Okay.'

Jack was laughing and Anthony was smiling as he said goodbye to his mother, acknowledged her effusive thanks with a modest nod and then left the room.

He didn't look back at Elsie.

CHAPTER TEN

ANTHONY HADN'T EVEN looked at her when he left Jack's room and it had made Elsie feel almost like a piece of the furniture.

And he'd been *smiling*.

Happy. As if being 'kind of friends' was perfectly okay.

And it was for her too. But only because it had to be. Elsie's heart felt as heavy as a piece of furniture for the rest of her shift. She helped Jack and his mother pack all his belongings and then his dad arrived to take them home and other staff gathered to wave them off and celebrate what really had been a miraculous survival and recovery story. They'd be talking about his case for a long time and it was already tucked into Elsie's memory banks, along with the fact that it had been Anthony who'd done the daunting and delicate surgery needed to save the boy who'd speared his heart with a metal rod.

It was another connection between them. Another addition to the weight of what was missing from her life now.

What could have been if they'd just happened to meet, perhaps, and neither of them had any baggage from their past lives?

Elsie's breath came out in a huff, as if she was laughing at herself, when she was changing out of her scrubs and into her civvies when her shift ended. As if anybody their age didn't have an entire trailer-load of baggage that had to be dragged along behind them. It was a bit over the top that she and Anthony shared a grandchild, but if they didn't Elsie knew they would never have connected in the first place. Not on the kind of level they had, anyway, because Anthony's baggage meant that he would never have trusted anyone to that extent.

And that trust would still be there, even if they were only friends, wouldn't it? If she could just get over missing him so much on a deeper level, they could end up being the best of friends, rather than just 'kind of friends' and they could be there for each other for support as well as sharing family times.

Coincidentally, it was Elsie's closest family member whose name came up on the screen of her phone as she walked into the section of St Nick's car park where her little, bright blue hatchback was waiting.

'Hey…' She tried to sound much brighter than she was actually feeling. 'Everything okay, love?' She opened her car door and threw her bag onto the passenger seat before getting in. 'How did the riding lesson go for Felix today?'

'It's still going. He's learning how to groom Bonnie so we'll be here for ages. And then we're meeting Jonno for hamburgers. I… I just needed a moment away from him so I could call you.'

Elsie's breath caught in her chest as she heard the undercurrent of emotion in her daughter's words. Something was seriously wrong. With Felix? With her relationship with Jonno?

'Tell me what's wrong,' she said gently. 'I'm sure, whatever it is, it's not as bad as you're thinking.'

'But it is.' Brie's indrawn breath was a strangled sob. 'I'm pregnant, Mum…'

* * *

Elsie was still sitting in her car, with her head bent and her eyes closed, almost an hour later.

The knock on her window wasn't loud but it was certainly enough to make her nearly jump out of her skin. Her heart was racing as her eyes snapped open to find that it was Anthony knocking on her window.

His face was a picture of apology.

'Sorry,' he said loudly enough for her to hear through the window. 'I didn't want to give you a fright but…' He shook his head and walked around her car to open the passenger door. 'Can I get in for a minute?' he asked. 'I've…um…just been talking to Jonno.'

Elsie pulled her shoulder bag from the seat by way of giving permission for Anthony to get in, but it felt as if the new hurdle in the lives of the people she loved the most had just become even more real and urgent because Anthony obviously knew about the pregnancy as well.

'He'd been at his gym,' Anthony said as he sat down. 'He said he'd needed a session on the toughest run of the climbing wall to try and clear his head, but it hadn't worked and he needed to talk to someone before he went to meet Brie and Felix. I'm guessing you've heard the news too?'

Elsie nodded. Brie had told her everything that had happened since she'd done the pregnancy test and told Jonno the result. That she'd walked out on him after telling him that an unplanned pregnancy was the last thing she'd wanted to happen. That she couldn't even think about it yet, let alone talk about it. It had been a relief that she'd had the excuse of needing to collect Felix from school and take him for his lesson at Riding for the Disabled and she'd hoped talking to her mother would help her get her head around the news.

And Jonno had been to talk to his father, which was another step in the trust they were building as they strengthened their relationship, and that was something Elsie knew she should be celebrating, but right now that seemed irrelevant. And on top of the emotional overload she was already dealing with, having Anthony so close to her in a confined space after keeping their distance so carefully for the last couple of weeks was almost overwhelming. She could even catch a whiff of that familiar, delicious scent of his skin and hair. She had to force herself to focus.

'How does *he* feel about the pregnancy?'

she asked. 'I don't think Brie's given him a chance to say anything yet.'

'He's over the moon. He said he'd never thought he'd want a family at all, but he fell in love with Felix pretty much the moment he met him and he couldn't love Brie any more than he does, so having another baby with her is like a gift. And this time he'll be there for the whole journey. The pregnancy. The birth. Watching the baby grow and celebrating every milestone. All those things he missed out on last time.'

Elsie swallowed hard. She could understand that. She could sense that Anthony was just as thrilled at the idea of sharing all the important moments of the life of a new grandchild from this moment on but…

Anthony said it for her. 'But Jonno thinks it's the last thing that Brie wanted to happen. You're right, she wouldn't even talk to him about it and he's…well… I think he's scared that she might not be able to cope. He's really worried about her but he doesn't know how to fix it.'

'*Fix* it?' Elsie shook her head. 'This isn't something that can be fixed. Brie's terrified. She knew Jonno wanted another child and she felt like she was letting him down but she couldn't face it. Not again.' Her heart was breaking for what she knew her daughter was going through at the moment. 'And she shouldn't have to.'

'So how did it happen?' Anthony sounded puzzled. 'I can understand the one accidental pregnancy that happened with Felix, but *two*?'

Elsie felt herself bristling. 'Brie was on the pill the night she met Jonno. She'd been on the pill for months to regulate her periods because they were so irregular it was a real problem. She got sick which made the contraception fail so it was hardly her fault.'

'I wasn't saying it was.'

Elsie ignored him. 'She went off the pill while she was pregnant, of course, and never went back on, even though her cycle was still irregular when it finally came back. She wasn't keen to be taking something on a permanent basis if she didn't really have to. I don't know how it happened this time. Or when but, you know, there are two people involved here. The responsibility—or blame—isn't just on Brie.'

'Blame?' Anthony was staring at her. 'You're making this sound like it's a catastrophe. This might be an unplanned pregnancy but it's not an unwanted one, by any means. Not by the father, anyway.'

'It's too much for Brie,' Elsie snapped. 'She's got more than enough on her plate at the moment. She's just got married. She's settling into a new career and a new house. She's already got a disabled child to care for.'

'Now you're making it sound like it's a given that she's going to have another disabled child.' Anthony gave his head a single shake as he corrected himself. 'That *they're* going to have another disabled child.'

'That's what she's scared of.'

'But the odds of that happening are very small. Four percent, Jonno said, and it can be picked up in a scan as early as about eleven weeks. How far along is she?'

'She doesn't know. Looking back, she said she's felt a bit off and tired for weeks but she put it down to the stress of moving and getting settled. They're making an appointment as soon as possible with the obstetrician who delivered Felix.' Elsie pulled in a deep breath. 'Do you really think it's that easy? That if you find out something is wrong with your baby you can just pull the plug and get rid of the problem?'

'I'm not suggesting any of it is easy. I'm just saying—'

But Elsie hadn't finished what *she* wanted to say. 'We didn't find out until Brie was twenty weeks along with Felix. She'd already been feeling her baby moving for a couple of weeks. But it wouldn't have made any difference if we'd found out even a couple of months earlier. We loved him from the moment we knew he existed, after we'd got over the surprise of it all. And you can't possibly know how much of a shock it was for her to be offered a termination. Or how hard it was for me to be the only person Brie had for support and to wonder whether I was doing the right thing in helping her in what felt like a fight to do the best thing for her baby. My grandbaby.'

'Mine too,' Anthony said quietly.

'You weren't there.' Elsie knew her words were cutting but she couldn't swallow them. 'You have no idea.' She put her hand over her eyes. 'It wasn't just the pregnancy. Or the surgery he had months before he was born and the waiting to see if the pregnancy would even last. There's been all the surgeries since. All the hospital visits and specialist appointments and knowing that any pain

he's going through won't be the last. The fear
that something worse could happen and that
might mean we could lose him. Or he won't
get the kind of future he deserves to have—
it's there like a cloud on the horizon. Even if
we manage to not think about it, we know it's
there, every minute of every day…'

Elsie's voice trailed into silence. It wasn't
just Brie who was terrified of the thought of
going through it all again. For a long moment
there was silence in the car and then Anthony
spoke quietly.

'I'm here now. So is Jonno. And we would
have been there for Felix if we'd known. We
were there, both of us, when he was sick
enough to be in danger last time. We will
be here from now on. Both of us. For every
minute of every day if that's what's needed.'

'I know.' Elsie bit her lip. She could hear
echoes of the impassioned words she'd just
thrown at Anthony and she knew it wasn't
fair. She could almost feel the distance between them increasing, despite how close
they were sitting in this small vehicle. It felt
as if some of those threads of connection between herself and Anthony were fraying and
breaking.

Or being deliberately cut?

'I'm sorry,' she said. 'This is a bit of a shock. Right now, all I can think about is trying to support my daughter. I know how scared she is and we're programmed to protect our children, aren't we?'

'Indeed,' Anthony agreed. 'And my son is just as much a part of this as your daughter.'

She met his gaze then and that feeling of distance went up another notch but it wasn't enough to kill that ability to communicate silently.

Are we taking sides here?

Are we going to stand by our own offspring on any battleground if it turns out that unbearable decisions have to be made?

What about Felix? Will he be in the middle of some ghastly tug-of-war?

It couldn't be allowed to happen.

'I think I've said enough.' Elsie turned to look through the windscreen. 'Too much, probably. I need to go home.'

'Of course.' Anthony reached for the door handle. 'I agree that there's probably nothing else that needs to be said at the moment. Not until we know more.' He opened the door but then hesitated before climbing out. 'I want to do everything I can to support Brie as well as

Jonno,' he said. 'And you too, Elsie,' he added quietly. 'I want you to know that.'

She nodded. But she didn't turn her head to look at him as he got out of the car and the door clicked shut behind him.

Had she really thought such a short time ago that they could end up being the best of friends and able to be there to support each other as well as sharing family times?

Right now that felt like as much of a fantasy as being in an intimate relationship with the man she'd fallen in love with.

Elsie put her bag back onto the passenger seat, trying to ignore the heat she could feel from the fabric that had been supporting Anthony's body. She fastened her seat belt and started the car, focusing on her driving enough for everything else swirling in her head to get pushed behind a safety barrier.

At some point on the route home, however, she felt something new merging with the weight of sadness that had been all about missing Anthony. It was almost a touch of relief, in a way. An acknowledgement that if choosing sides in supporting their children was breaking that very personal connection between them, it would make it a lot easier being in each other's company going forward.

Especially for something like going on a shared holiday.

Or would the rapidly approaching 'familymoon' get cancelled as this new development, with all its dangerous undercurrents, meant that being together could become an emotional whirlpool they would all prefer to avoid?

This was why the relationship between them had had to end.

Marriages and families were complicated enough without adding a dimension that could fuel the flames and increase the intensity of any crisis. It was automatic that they would both try and see any situation from their own child's point of view. They might be coming from opposite ends of the spectrum—Elsie had been overprotective of Brie since before her daughter had even been born and they couldn't be closer, whereas Anthony was only beginning to forge the kind of relationship he had been denied for decades—but the end result was the same. It was creating a gulf between them.

How much worse would it be now if they had still been in that close, secret relationship? Being forced apart on a personal level by how they were reacting to Brie's unexpected pregnancy but also being held together because they both needed to support their families.

Family.

Ironically, they had got to know each other and become so close because they were part of the same family, but it was *because* they were part of the same family that the relationship couldn't have been allowed to continue.

And that was why Anthony shouldn't be where he was, right now—on the doorstep of his old family home. Not when he was perfectly well aware that Elsie was going to be here babysitting Felix while his parents went to the appointment with the ultrasound technician who specialised in advanced techniques for diagnosing foetal abnormalities.

But it was well past the time he'd expected to hear some news. Maybe Jonno had simply forgotten to turn his phone back on after the appointment this afternoon, but if that wasn't the case and they still weren't home he knew that Elsie would be on tenterhooks just as much as he was.

More so, perhaps. Because, as she'd pointed out so clearly, he hadn't been there the first time so he couldn't actually have any idea how awful it had been for both Brie and Elsie.

He *had* been there, however, when Felix had been unwell enough for them all to be worried sick. When he knew his support had been something Elsie had appreciated. When those first connections had been made. Connections that had steadily deepened and strengthened until he'd thought he'd found someone he could trust enough to… Well, he hadn't been brave enough to get as far as imagining the shape that a future with Elsie Henderson might have. He'd given up on the idea of marriage, so long ago that it wasn't a consideration, but he'd known he was in love with her and, given how much he'd missed her in recent weeks, being simply friends was definitely not what he'd begun dreaming of.

So he'd come here instead of tackling that overdue paperwork in his office or going home to pace the polished floors of his apartment. And when it was Elsie that answered his knock on the door he could see instantly that he'd been right in thinking she would be unbearably anxious.

'Oh, no…' she said as she opened the door. 'Have you heard something? Are they…? Is it...?' She couldn't find the words for what she needed to know.

'I haven't heard anything,' Anthony told her quickly. 'I thought I'd drop by just in case they were home already.'

Elsie shook her head. For a moment she seemed to be clinging to Anthony's gaze, as if she needed something that she knew he could provide.

Strength perhaps?

Yes. He would always be able to do that for Elsie. 'We'll hear soon,' he said. 'And it's going to be okay.'

Oh, man... As a doctor he knew better than to offer reassurance that could not be guaranteed. Except that he meant this.

'Whatever the result,' he added softly. 'We'll take it one step at a time and we'll manage. It *will* be okay.'

He saw the way Elsie took a gulp of air as she nodded. He could also see the way those anxious lines around her eyes softened just a little and he felt his heart squeeze as he realised she was accepting his support.

That she needed him, even?

'Would you like to come in and wait?' she asked, stepping back. Then she shook her head. 'How weird is this? Me inviting you into the house that's been your home for most of your life?'

Anthony smiled. 'Everything's a bit weird at the moment, isn't it?'

Elsie's cheeks were pink and she wasn't meeting his gaze. 'I'm sorry about the other day. I shouldn't have said a lot of what I said.'

'You were upset.' Anthony took his coat off and, without thinking, hooked it over the large decorative wooden acorn on top the newel post at the bottom of the staircase, just like he always had. 'I do understand.'

'Would you like a cup of tea? Or something stronger?' Elsie glanced at her watch. 'I reckon the sun's over the yardarm.' There was a hint of a smile curving her lips. 'And even if it isn't I don't think it matters right now.'

'Sounds like a great idea to me.' Anthony nodded. 'What's Felix up to?'

'He's watching his new favourite movie. You know the one about the zebra who grows up to become a racehorse?'

'No.'

'I'm sure you'll get to know it very soon. You can go and catch the end of it now, if you want to?'

Anthony shook his head. 'I'd rather have

a glass of wine with you.' He raised an eye-brow. 'If that's okay…?'

'Of course.'

Anthony couldn't interpret the tone in Elsie's words as she led the way into the kitchen but it seemed almost businesslike. And then it brightened. 'Let's see if the kids have got anything nice that's already cold.' She threw a glance over her shoulder as she opened the fridge. 'I expected Jonno and Brie home ages ago. Why do you think it's taking so long?'

'It could be that they were running late to start with, but it's a very detailed assessment so it was always going to be a long appointment.'

'Can't they see instantly if there's an abnormality in the spine?' Elsie pulled out a half empty bottle of wine. 'Is a Pinot Gris okay? Or there'll be a bottle of red wine somewhere, I'm sure.'

'White's fine. And I'm sure Jonno won't mind if we finish that off.' Anthony took his glass and went to sit on an old couch that was positioned against the wall close to one set of French windows to provide a view of the lovely garden stretching beyond the flagged terrace.

'It's more complicated than simply checking the baby's back,' he told Elsie. 'Especially at this early stage of development. It's more to do with precise measurements of intracranial anatomy like the posterior fossa. The translucency is important as well. Even the shape of the head at this stage can be an indicator for a neural tube defect like spina bifida.'

Elsie had come to sit beside him. 'You sound like you know a lot about it.'

Anthony let his breath out in a sigh. 'I confess I've been reading all the latest information I could find ever since we spoke the other day.'

'So you're worried too.' Elsie took a mouthful of her drink. 'Even though the blood test showed that Brie's level of Alpha-fetoprotein is only slightly raised?'

Anthony caught Elsie's gaze and held it just that bit longer than he knew he should. Maybe because it kind of felt like he was holding her hand?

'Worrying is part of the job description of any parent, isn't it?'

Elsie seemed as reluctant as he was to break the eye contact. 'And grandparent,' she added. 'But I do wish they'd call.'

'Jonno said they're hoping that their doctor will be available to go over the results with them straight away. Maybe that's what's keeping them so long.' Anthony took a swallow of his wine. 'It's kind of lucky that Brie's cycle has always been so irregular, in a way. We might have had to wait a lot longer if she hadn't already been so far along by the time she did the test. And we're even luckier that the technology's so advanced now. 3D and transvaginal scanning make early detection a lot more accurate.'

He leaned back on the soft cushions of the couch as they both sat in silence for a while.

'I've always loved this room,' he said then. 'Which is funny because I was hardly ever in it. I love it even more now, though. Maybe it takes a happy family to make a kitchen really come alive.'

'That's true. It's where you make the food to nurture the people you love. Where you come together to share it. I guess you used the dining room here more than the kitchen?'

'We rarely ate together,' Anthony admitted. 'Unless it was a formal dinner party. I think Jonno always had his meals in here. With his nanny.' It had been another area of that unhappy marriage that he'd been taught not to interfere with.

'It's different now.' Elsie smiled. 'And we get to share it sometimes.'

Like the last time they'd been here together? At the barbecue that had ended with the realisation that their relationship couldn't continue. Anthony tried to distract himself by letting his gaze roam around the room. There were pictures held onto the front of the fridge by magnets and one of them looked like a portrait of a wolf that Felix had created with felt pens. The animal had bright yellow eyes and an extraordinary number of teeth.

'I can't believe how different it feels,' he agreed. 'Or how lucky I am to share it.' He cleared his throat. 'Can I confess something else?'

Elsie looked startled. Wary? Did she think he was going to say something about missing what they'd discovered they could give each other?

At least he could reassure her that he wasn't about to step on forbidden ground.

'I hate where I'm living,' he told her. 'Even if it was never like it is now, this old house always felt far more like a home than that apartment ever will.'

Elsie opened her mouth to say something,

but in the same instant they heard the sound of the front door opening.

Anthony could sense that they were both holding their breath as they listened to the footsteps on the tiled hallway floor getting closer. He took Elsie's glass and put it by his own on the table as they both stood up to face the internal door of the kitchen. Brie came in first and she looked tired. And pale. Jonno was right behind her and he put his arm around his wife's shoulders as soon as she stopped.

For a long, long moment, nobody said anything. And then Jonno cleared his throat.

'It's fine,' he told them. 'Everything's perfectly normal.' His voice caught and Brie looked up at him so they were looking at each other as he finished speaking. 'It's a girl,' he said softly. 'We're going to have a baby girl and she's going to be fine…'

There were hugs that needed to be had. A celebration of the kind that could bind families together tightly enough to last for ever, but for just a moment longer neither Anthony nor Elsie moved an inch. They too were sharing a glance and Anthony could see how enormous the relief was that Elsie was feeling. The love for her family, including the new baby girl on the way, was almost blinding but Anthony thought he could see something else there as well.

That a part of that limitless love was his. And his alone.

That Elsie was just as much in love with him as he was with her.

It should have been heartbreaking, but nothing could dampen the joy of this moment. Especially when Felix came into the kitchen to see what all the noise was about and he was finally told that he was going to get a baby sister in the not too distant future.

His face lit up. 'I knew I would,' he exclaimed. 'I didn't change my wish into something about the wolfs even when I said I was going to.' He was almost dancing in his excitement. 'Did you see the picture I did, Grandpa? It's on the fridge.'

'I did. I love your wolf's teeth.'

'We're going to see them. It's…how many sleeps now, Mumma?'

'Nine,' Brie told him. 'Single figures already.'

'So we're still going to go?' Elsie had crouched down to hug Felix.

'Why not? I'm pregnant, Mum, not sick.' Brie was looking at Jonno again and the love between them was such a solid thing that Anthony could swear it was visible. 'And what better way to celebrate this than by having a familymoon?'

'We'll keep Mumma safe from the wolves, won't we, Felix?' Jonno scooped his son up into his arms.

The solemn nod from the little boy as he wrapped his arms around his father's neck brought a lump to Anthony's throat. So did the way Brie caught her mother's gaze and they exchanged misty smiles.

He was part of this. This was *his* family.

And it was everything he could have ever dreamed of. Until Elsie's gaze brushed his own and he felt a part of his heart that wasn't open enough to absorb that joy.

But it was almost everything he could have ever dreamed of. And it was more than he'd ever had before so it was enough.

It had to be enough.

CHAPTER ELEVEN

THIS WAS AS good as it got.

The sun was still shining late in the afternoon when the Morgan/Henderson family set out to explore the small French town that would be their home for the next few days. The flight had been smooth and swift and the spectacular views as they'd landed, with mountains towering on one side and the deep blue of the Mediterranean sea sparkling on the other, had already set the bar high for the best holiday ever.

Jonno drove the rental car the short distance to Villefranche-sur-Mer and they stayed in their luxurious accommodation just long enough to unpack what they needed and admire the huge terrace and sea views before setting off on foot to explore a place that their guidebook promised would be unforgettable.

They had known they would need to navigate steep hills and many steps as they wandered towards the sea, admiring picture-perfect pastel-coloured houses and cobbled streets with hanging baskets of bright flowers, but Felix and Jonno had already made a plan.

'Dadda's going to be a real-life Nobby,' Felix told them. 'I can ride on his back when it's too bumpy in my chair.'

With his toy horse Nobby tucked firmly under his arm, that was exactly the perfect way to go sightseeing. His small wheelchair was light enough to be easily pushed when it was empty and Anthony took responsibility for it when Jonno was giving his son a piggyback. They naturally fell into a pattern where Brie walked beside Jonno and Anthony walked behind the younger couple with Elsie beside him, happily taking far too many photographs.

They explored the sixteenth century citadel and then headed for the old town along the harbour road to find a restaurant for dinner so that they could get Felix to bed at a reasonable hour.

'Oh, look…' Elsie exclaimed. 'What a gorgeous chapel.'

The tiny building was on the sea side of the

road, painted in soft earthy colours and richly decorated with various patterns.

'It's got *eyes*.' Felix lifted one of his hands from his father's head to point.

'It's the chapel of Saint Pierre,' Anthony told them, scrolling through the information he'd found almost instantly on his phone. 'He's the patron saint of fishermen and the eyes are there to watch over the fishermen and keep them safe when they're out at sea. And look, Felix. Can you see what the cross on the steeple is made of?'

Elsie took a photograph of the three generations of Morgans peering up at the steeple. How could Anthony have ever believed he wasn't Jonno's biological father? The family resemblance was unmistakable. Even the way they were all squinting in the fading sunlight, their heads tilted to the same side, was identical. Brie had obviously seen it too because she was laughing. She also had one hand resting gently on her belly and the reminder that a precious new baby was on its way to join this family made Elsie feel as if her heart was so full of joy it was in danger of bursting.

'Can you see, darling?' she asked Felix. 'It's four fish that are joined together to make the cross. Isn't that cool?'

But Felix had had enough of sightseeing for now. 'I'm hungry,' he announced.

They found a restaurant on the flat waterfront with outdoor seating beneath an awning, an enchanting view of the harbour dotted with small boats and plenty of room for a wheelchair. There were fairy lights that trailed from the awning into the branches of trees filling big terracotta pots and a child-friendly menu that included pizza and lasagne.

'We are almost on the Italian border,' Jonno said. 'But I don't reckon the lasagne will be as good as yours, Elsie.'

'I'm going to eat something French,' Brie said.

'Like snails?' Jonno laughed.

'Don't be silly, Dadda,' Felix chided. 'Nobody eats *snails*.'

For a split second, as Elsie caught Anthony's gaze in the burst of laughter, she completely forgot that she needed to keep her distance. Or that that distance had increased all too easily when they'd both stepped into their own corners to protect their own children. They'd both felt the same overwhelming relief at the reassuring news about their unborn grandchild's development and they were both determined to make this family holiday a celebration of their new—and grow-ing—family.

But how romantic was this? A setting sun and a harbour view. Fairy lights and cob-bled streets. The sound of the most beautiful language in the world around them, classic French music coming from a sound system nearby and a tall flute of the champagne An-thony had ordered already in her hand.

So…just for that moment, Elsie let herself hold Anthony's gaze for longer than she knew she should and he didn't look away. He held up his glass to touch hers instead, and they shared a smile that shut the rest of the world away for a heartbeat and then another—because Anthony seemed to want this contact that was like no other. Physical but without touching. Intimate but perfectly acceptable in public. Something that could only happen with two people who cared for each other far more than any kind of 'friend'. The thought that Anthony might, in fact, be missing her as much as she was missing him filled El-sie's heart even further and it was aching by the time she took a sip of her champagne and opened her menu as though food was upper-most in her mind.

It was only then that she noticed an odd

note in the silence at the table and she glanced sideways just in time to catch Brie looking down at her menu—as if she didn't want to make eye contact with her mother.

As if she'd noticed something more than a friendly toast to a shared holiday that she had just exchanged with Anthony?

Oh, help...

Elsie felt a tiny shiver slither down her spine. This was a wake-up call, that was what it was. She couldn't afford to let her guard down for even a moment. Not even if they were in the most romantic country ever.

Not even if it seemed that Anthony would be just as happy to close that distance.

'Haven't you noticed anything? Anything at all?'

'Can't say I have.' Jonno was watching Felix, who had his nose pressed against a glass panel on the raised deck which was one of the many viewing platforms in the wolf park.

'What about last night, at dinner? The way Mum was looking at your dad at the table.' Brie shook her head. 'It reminded me of when I was just little and she got the photograph albums out and told me stories about *my* dad and how wonderful he was and she'd get all misty and cry sometimes.'

'Guess I was too busy choosing my dinner,' Jonno said. 'How good was that steak and the mashed potatoes with truffles?' He grinned at Brie. 'I'm glad I didn't go for the snails just to horrify Felix. And then we all went to bed early, didn't we? We knew we'd need a bit of stamina for today's adventures.'

But Brie wasn't going to be distracted. She'd been thinking about this during the spectacular drive up through pretty villages and forests and gorges carved into cliffs above the river to get this close to the Italian border in the Alps. She'd hardly taken in any of the information in the introductory session in the old stone stable either, although she was aware that there were three wolf packs in the park and Felix was currently waiting for the feeding session to begin with the Canadian wolf pack.

After that they had a busy few hours planned at the park. They were going to a falconry show to see owls and eagles and vultures perform with their handlers, give Felix time to explore the attractive children's playground, have lunch in the café or a picnic in a designated area of the forest and then catch another feeding session with a different wolf pack later this afternoon. No doubt Felix would be sound asleep in the car by the time they headed back to the coast, especially since he'd been up since the crack of dawn with the excitement of this long-awaited trip to the wolf park becoming a reality at last.

Brie saw Anthony pointing at something in the trees and caught a glimpse of something pale moving behind the tree trunks. She saw Felix shake his head sadly, however, letting Anthony know he hadn't seen it, so his grandfather scooped him up to hold him higher. Now it was Elsie who was pointing and a few seconds later Felix was clapping his hands with excitement. But Brie wasn't scanning the forest again or watching for the park rangers who would be coming out with chunks of meat in a bucket to feed the wolves. No...

She was watching her mother. And the way Elsie was watching Anthony as he held his grandson safely in his arms.

'I think she likes him,' she muttered. 'In fact, I'm sure of it.'

'What's not to like?' Jonno draped his arm around her shoulders. 'Like father, like son. Or should I say like son, like father? I'll bet he likes her too. Like daughter, like mother.'

He pulled Brie a little closer but she nudged him gently with her elbow. 'We talked about this. How weird it would be if our parents liked each other. As in, you know…*liked* each other.'

'Like we do, you mean?' Jonno's gaze was soft as he held hers. Then he bent his head and kissed her. And Brie kissed him back. How could she not? She'd never been this happy in her life.

And she wanted the people she loved to be just as happy.

'What if they heard us that night? When we were joking about it while we did the dishes? When we said we might have to toss a coin to see which grandparent got to come to a birthday party or Christmas dinner?'

'Well…it could be a bit awkward if they ended up not wanting to talk to each other.'

'But what if we stopped something happening that might make them as happy as *we* are?'

'You've got a point. It's not as if Dad had anything like a good marriage the first time round and I didn't exactly make life any happier for him for a long time, did I?' Jonno raised an eyebrow. 'Do you think we should encourage it? Send *them* out for a romantic dinner tonight while *we* babysit Felix, instead of the other way round?'

'That might be a bit obvious.' Brie had a more subtle idea. 'Why don't I sit in front with you on the drive home, instead of being in the back with Mum and Felix?' She bit her lip. 'No one else can drive because the rental car is under your licence and being in the front seat might help me not to feel car sick on all those bendy bits in the gorges. You know…the way pregnant women can get?'

Jonno's face softened even more. And then he kissed her again. 'I love you,' he murmured. 'Even if you are a devious match-maker.'

Felix had turned in his grandfather's arms to search for his parents. 'They're coming, Mumma. The man with the wolfs' lunch. Come and see, Dadda… *Quick…*'

Jonno was already moving closer to the window but his smile advertised that he'd caught Brie's mouthed words.

'Love you too…'

Felix was almost asleep by the time the straps of his car seat were clicked into place, so it wasn't surprising that Brie suggested she sat in the front beside Jonno. Not that Elsie had noticed her daughter feeling queasy on the tight curves and tunnels in the road through the gorges on the way up to the mountains but it was a perfectly reasonable swap and she certainly wasn't going to complain about seeing more than the back of Anthony's head on the journey.

It had been a perfect day and it turned out that the timing had also been perfect because there were some rather dramatic dark clouds gathering above the mountain peaks and it looked as if they might be in for a storm.

'Maybe we should go straight home and not stop in any more of the villages,' Jonno suggested. 'I've heard that the storms in this part of France can be quite violent.'

Anthony was nodding. 'They hit the news quite often. With floods and hailstones the size of golf balls.'

'Oh, stop…' Elsie said. 'I'm sure we'll get home well before it arrives.'

Brie laughed. 'And I reckon Felix will sleep through any size of hailstones. He's *so* tired…'

'And *so* happy.' Jonno smiled as he glanced sideways at Brie. 'Could be that everything else on this trip is going to be an anti-climax after the "wolfs".'

Or maybe not.

The enormous clouds, with inky black centres and eerily bright edges as they did their best to block the sun, were filling the sky by the time they reached one of the narrowest parts of the road, with a stone wall on the cliff side and the river, with its churning white rapids, only metres away down the bank on the other. A few heavy drops of rain hit the windscreen and Jonno reached to turn on the wipers. The first crack of thunder was terrifyingly loud, so close the flash of lightning came simultaneously and the combined effect of both the sound and light was enough for them to feel it vibrating in their bones.

And it all happened in a blink of time, too fast for Jonno to be able to do anything to prevent it. A truck coming around the curve ahead of them was suddenly on the wrong side of the road and there was simply nowhere for him to go to try and avoid a head-on collision. Into the cliff on the right or towards the riverbank on the left? With his ability to analyse and respond to emergencies, Jonno must have realised in that nanosecond of time that they stood more chance heading towards the open side than becoming a sandwich between a much heavier vehicle and a wall of stone. He pulled on the steering wheel and started to brake at almost the same time but a second bolt of lightning, followed instantly by the crack of thunder, split the weird darkness outside and covered the scream of...who was it?

Brie?

Felix?

Elsie twisted within her seat belt as she turned to put her arms around Felix to protect him, only to find that Anthony's arms were already there. The car tipped and bounced and cracked against what felt like rocks. Elsie could feel Anthony holding *her* as well as providing an extra layer of protection for Felix but she kept her eyes squeezed shut so tightly she could only see stars, convinced that these were her last moments on earth. It took only seconds but it felt like for ever and then numerous airbags went off with sounds even more frightening than the thunder.

'*Mumma...*' Felix was screaming beneath his grandparents' tight hold. '*Dadda...*'

'It's okay, buddy. I'm coming to get you.'

Jonno's voice was astonishingly calm and Elsie's eyes snapped open. The car was still rocking but it was staying in one place.

And they were still alive.

'Brie?' There was an urgency in Jonno's voice now. 'Does anything hurt? Take a deep breath for me, hon.'

'I'm...okay...' But there was panic in Brie's voice. 'There's water around my feet. Jonno... we're *in* the river. We've got to get out. We've got to get Felix out.'

But Jonno took another second to assess their predicament.

'Dad? Elsie? Are you okay? Felix?'

'Dadda...' Felix was sobbing. 'I want to get *out*. I don't like this car...'

'Elsie?' It was Anthony asking this time. He was reaching to touch her face. 'You're not hurt, are you?'

'I don't think so.' But then Elsie tried to move and cried out in pain. 'My foot...' she said. 'I can't move it. I think it's caught under the front seat.'

'I can't get this door open.' Jonno had taken off his seat belt. He was holding the door catch open and trying to thump the frame with his shoulder. 'And the window control isn't working.'

'I'll try mine.' Brie reached for her door but Jonno stopped her.

'Don't. We have to get out this side. The rapids are too close.'

Elsie was undoing the clips of Felix's safety belts so that she could gather him into her arms and cuddle him to try and stop the heartbreaking sobbing.

'It's okay, darling,' she told him, over and over. 'We'll get out really soon.'

There were people climbing down the bank beside them now and she could hear them shouting. On the road above, traffic had come to a standstill and the vehicles' headlights were shining into the sheets of rain now falling.

Anthony was pushing the button beside the headrest on the driver's seat and pulling it upwards. 'Use the spikes on the bottom,' he told Jonno as he passed the headrest through the gap between the front seats. 'Break the window.'

Was it the effort Jonno was putting into smashing the glass that made the back of the car grind and slip on the boulders that had caught them in the shallow edge of this fast-moving river? Elsie saw the flash of fear in Anthony's eyes as he looked past her to the foaming rapids that were far too close and she knew that, while they had survived the crash, they would not survive the car being caught and swept away by the river's current. She cuddled Felix even closer so that he couldn't see that she was crying with fear herself.

The car window broke and shattered, tiny pieces of the safety glass showering Jonno, but he kept going as fast as he could, to get more of the pieces still clinging to the frame. A man outside was helping. They were talking to Jonno but it quickly became obvious that he didn't understand. Another man came closer.

'Help is coming,' he said in English. 'We must get you out.'

Jonno twisted. 'Pass me Felix,' he ordered.

'*No…*' Felix clung to Elsie, even as Jonno reached back to get hold of his son.

It was one of the hardest things Elsie had ever done to prise Felix's arms from around her neck and push him towards Jonno. He dragged him through the gap between the seats and then through the window into the arms of the people outside, who were standing almost knee-deep in water, amongst slippery rocks, in a chain leading back to the firm ground of a narrow shoreline at the base of the bank.

'You're next, Brie.'

'But I can't… There's no room… You'll have to get out first.' And then Brie turned to the back of the car, her face scrunched into lines of terror. '*Mum*... Have you got your foot free?'

'Yes.' It was a lie, but the only thing Elsie was concerned with right now was that her daughter got safely out of this car. 'It's okay, love. You get out. I'll be right behind you.'

Jonno had squeezed himself out of the window and was reaching back to catch and help Brie. She could hear Brie's groan as she squeezed herself through the narrow gap of the window frame but she couldn't afford to add any fear about the baby Brie was carrying to her state of mind just yet. There was too much else to be frightened about.

Jonno was halfway back through the window as soon as others had taken over supporting Brie to safety. 'I can reach the lever on the seat,' he told Anthony. 'If you come into the front, we can push the back of the seat flat and it'll make it easier for us to get to Elsie.'

Elsie tried again to pull her foot free but it was stuck fast. It felt as if sharp edges of metal were biting into her skin as she pulled even harder. She had to give up and in that moment she felt the front of the car, now much lighter, swing sideways and the whole vehicle rocked as the waves of the rapids tried to snare it.

Elsie could hear the sound of a helicopter hovering overhead already and there were even some flashing lights of emergency vehicles on the road above them now, but were any rescuers going to be too late?

'You have to get out,' she told Anthony. 'Quick... I think the car's going to be washed away.'

'Come out, Dad.' Jonno's voice was a command. 'I'll get in and see how I can get that foot free. There's someone with a crowbar and a police car is here. They're saying a fire truck is not far away.'

But Anthony didn't move. He was holding Elsie's hand very tightly. 'I'm not going anywhere,' he told her. 'Not until I know you're safe.'

Amazingly, amongst all that terror, there was something wonderful to be found. That look in Anthony's eyes.

The fear.

The *love*...

But then he let go of her hand. 'I'm going to see what I can feel under the seat,' he told her.

Elsie could feel his hand on her ankle and then on her foot. 'There's a spike of metal,' he called above an increasing sound of rushing water and shouting outside the vehicle. 'It's right through your shoe. I can't tell if it's in your foot because everything's twisted.'

'I'll come in,' Jonno said. 'Maybe I can use the crowbar to lift the seat.'

'I've got one end of the shoelace,' Anthony called back. 'I'm going to see if I can untie it and loosen the shoe but...it's all under water...'

So far under that Anthony's face was almost touching the water as he reached beneath the seat. The level was rising and the car felt less and less stable but there was nothing Elsie could do except focus all her energy on the man right beside her.

'Please...' she whispered. 'Please get out, Anthony... Save yourself...'

He either didn't hear her or was simply ignoring her. 'I've loosened the lace,' he shouted. 'And I'm going to hold your ankle and help you pull. Try again, Elsie...'

She pulled and felt her foot slip a little. She pulled again with Anthony's fingers a tight band adding extra weight. There was a flash of pain but her foot slipped further.

And then it was free. Anthony was upright in a heartbeat. He was pulling and then push-

ing her towards the window only seconds
later and Elsie held out her arms. It was Jonno
who caught them first and then there were
others as she felt her body squeeze through
the gap and into even more of the icy river
water. But she didn't feel safe yet. Not even
when she knew they were on solid ground.
She pushed at her rescuers and told them to
wait. To put her down.

She wasn't going to feel really safe until
she knew that Anthony was. She could see
that his head was out of the car window. That
he was holding onto Jonno's arms and that
his son had a firm grip on his father's upper
arms, but she could also see that the car was
moving. Swinging further into the rapids.
And then, in the space of time it took for
Elsie to realise she'd been holding her breath
for far too long, it happened. The car twisted
and then rolled, turning upside down and then
sinking as it got claimed by the vicious current of the rapids, and in that final dramatic
moment Anthony was pulled free. By his son.

She heard the cheer going up from what
was now quite a crowd of onlookers. There
were the flashing lights of more emergency
vehicles and she could see Brie and Felix
looking down on the scene, wrapped in blan-

kets and coats and the arms of total strangers. But then Jonno was beside her, his arm around his father's waist as he helped him out of the river, and suddenly there was only one place that Elsie needed to be.

In the arms of the man she loved.

And, judging by the way he was holding her, he was feeling exactly the same way...

CHAPTER TWELVE

THE STEADY BLIP-BLIP-BLIP was the best sound they had ever heard.

The sound of an unborn baby's heartbeat as part of an ultrasound that told them this tiny girl had been well protected in her mother's womb and by the technology of a modern car.

The only physical injury was to Elsie's foot, which was badly bruised after being half crushed and twisted in the seat mechanism. There were no broken bones but it was heavily bandaged and she had been sitting in a wheelchair ever since they had all been transferred to the hospital in Nice to be checked.

'Just like me,' Felix had told her approvingly. 'When my legs are tired.'

When their rescuers discovered that both Jonno and Brie worked for emergency services in England, that Anthony and Elsie were a doctor and nurse and that the little boy had the challenge of living with spina bifida they had all been treated like royalty. When they came out from the ultrasound exam there were still members of the French rescue team waiting to hear the results.

'The baby is fine,' Jonno told them. 'But we're going to cut our holiday short and go home so that we're close to our own doctors, just to be on the safe side.'

Jonno might be being overprotective of his wife and baby but nobody was going to argue with him. Elsie wanted to be in her own home, safe and sound, herself. The shock of coming so close to losing her life today was going to take a while to wear off.

'But you'll come back, yes?'

'Absolutely. As soon as we can.'

A smiling fireman stepped forward from the back of the group with something wrapped in a towel.

'This was found by the river after you went in the helicopter,' he told them. 'We thought it might be special.'

Felix's face lit up when the towel was unwrapped to reveal a still rather soggy toy.

He was still cuddling Nobby, sitting on Elsie's knee, as their well-wishers finally left, more than happy with the part they had played in a highly successful mission. 'I was going to wish for you when I went to bed,' Felix told the toy horse. 'Except I knew we didn't have any stars here.'

'There are always stars,' Anthony told him, crouching beside the wheelchair. 'Sometimes you can just feel them rather than see them but that doesn't mean you can't make a wish.'

Felix's eyes were wide. 'Do you wish on stars too, Grandpa?'

'I do.'

Felix tilted his head to look up at Elsie. 'Do *you* wish on stars too, Nana?'

'Sometimes,' she admitted. She didn't need to look up because Anthony was at eye level, having crouched down to talk to Felix.

'What do you wish for?'

Jonno and Brie exchanged a glance and Brie held out a hand to Felix. 'Let's go and find a taxi to take us home, shall we?'

But Felix shook his head. 'But I want to know.'

Elsie caught her lip between her teeth, but everybody seemed to be smiling and suddenly it felt as if it was about more than the sheer relief of a whole family having survived a potentially catastrophic accident.

It really did feel as if there were imaginary stars in the air around them. And that wishes could come true.

'We know,' Jonno said quietly to his father. 'You would have stayed in that car if we hadn't been able to get Elsie out, wouldn't you?'

'Yes.' The single word was raw.

Felix's eyes were very wide. 'Because you didn't want Nana to be lonely?'

'Because I love Nana,' Anthony said. 'Very, very much.'

Oh... Elsie could see the truth of that in Anthony's eyes and she could feel the truth of it. She just hoped he could see a reflection of that same kind of love in *her* eyes. For *him*. Because she wasn't going to find any words right at this moment.

Felix was nodding. 'I love Nana too,' he said.

'So do we,' Brie said. 'Which is why we need to leave her alone with Grandpa for a minute. Come on...'

Felix obediently slid off Elsie's lap but he

was scowling. 'I still want to know,' he muttered, 'what Nana's wish is.'

'I wish...' Elsie had to clear the lump from her throat. 'I wish that I could kiss Grandpa.'

Felix looked unimpressed. 'Why can't you?'

Brie and Jonno exchanged another meaningful glance. 'No reason at all,' Jonno said.

'We think it's a great idea, in fact,' Brie added. 'You're perfect for each other—just like your kids are.' She caught Felix's hand. 'Now, come *on*, bubba. We need to get Nobby home and dry before he catches a cold. And then we've got a plane to catch to really go home.'

It was just the two of them, then. Temporarily, anyway, because they'd need to follow their family soon and share the taxi to get back in time to gather their belongings and get to the airport again, but neither of them was in a hurry to move just yet.

Anthony laid his palm gently on Elsie's cheek without breaking the eye contact between them.

'I think it's a great idea too,' he said softly. 'I do love you, Elsie. So much. It's thanks to you that my life is as perfect as it's ever been but...but is it wrong to want more? To want to have you in my life as a lot more than just a friend?'

'If it's wrong, then I'm just as guilty.' Elsie was smiling. 'I love you too, Anthony, and I've been missing you *so* much. I think I fell in love with you the moment I saw how lost you were. When I knew you'd never been loved the way you deserve to be. The way I will always love you.'

Anthony was smiling but his eyes looked suspiciously bright. 'You know what?'

'What?'

'I'm about to make your wish come true.'

And he did. Although Elsie knew perfectly well that he was kissing her as much as she was kissing him. A soft kiss that was perfectly within any limits for a public place, but…oh…there was passion simmering beneath that softness. A desire that might need to be contained but they had plenty of time, didn't they? The rest of their lives might just be long enough…

She also knew that Brie had been right. She and Anthony *were* perfect for each other and they were lucky enough to be finding something as precious as this kind of love at a stage in their lives when it felt like no small miracle.

They broke the kiss to find a breath and to smile into each other's eyes. Maybe it was even better to find it now because they were old enough and wise enough to know they needed to make the most of every minute of every day they could spend with each other.

Starting right now.

With another kiss...

EPILOGUE

One year later...

IT WAS THE last day of the second 'family-moon' for the Morgans.

A holiday that had been jam-packed with adventures, including a whole day at the wolf park for seven-year-old Felix.

Five-month-old Bella had spent most of her time in the front pack that was her daddy's favourite new fashion accessory but, judging by the frequency of the baby's gurgling laughter and beaming smiles, she seemed to think her first family holiday was the best thing ever.

The bride and groom from the recent wedding were just as happy. The ceremony to celebrate Anthony and Elsie's commitment to each other had been held in the garden of the big old family homestead—the one with the pond that was so full of frogs. Elsie had worn the same silver dress she'd worn for her daughter's beach wedding and Brie, as her bridesmaid, had worn the same pretty green dress she'd got married in. It was Felix who'd begged to have the red bowties again and this time Anthony wore one too.

So did Bella, as a tiny velvet bow on a headband, nestled amongst her wispy dark curls. Everybody agreed she looked exactly like Felix at that age and, as a big brother, he couldn't have been prouder. He loved his little sister so much that he read her a bed-time story every day. The same story. And there was already a soft toy Nobby hidden in a cupboard to be ready for her first birthday.

There had been anxious times as well as so many happy ones, of course. Everybody had watched Brie like a hawk until she was well past the timeframe that could have revealed any problems the accident might have caused. Elsie had been off work for some time while her foot had healed, but Anthony had assured Felix that he wasn't letting Nana get lonely.

He would have been happy to move into Elsie's little terraced house, in fact, and couldn't wait to leave the apartment he hated, but she'd wanted them to start their life together somewhere that would be chosen by them both but completely new to them both as well. Somewhere they could be together for the rest of their lives with no ghosts from the past lurking anywhere.

They didn't want to be too far away from their family, because that was a huge part of their present and future, but they didn't want to live in each other's pockets either, so they'd bought a small cottage in a village on the outskirts of Bristol. Close enough to make it easy to keep working for as long as they wanted to, but far enough to be their very own space.

Just for them.

Because they were as much in love with each other as it was possible for a couple of any age to be and all lovers needed that kind of space.

To be alone.

Together...

* * * * *